The Price of Survival

From the Historian Tales

By Lance Conrad

To Makye,

12-16-19

DAWN STAR
PRESS

The Price of Survival

For information about discounts, bulk purchases, or reproduction of content in this book, please contact Dawn Star Press:

info@dawnstarpress.com

Cover art by William Thorup

ISBN: 978-0-9910230-8-0

Printed in the United States of America

For my lovely wife Erin,
who believes.

Chapter 1

I am the Historian. I am immortal. I am ageless. I am nameless. I am carried by my own feet through times and worlds to witness great stories.

This is one such story.

"At least it's starting to warm up a little," Kip commented. "The sun is out longer and longer each day."

"Yes," I nodded sagely, as if I really had some sense of this planet's seasons. Kip seemed to enjoy it when I acted old and wise, though I spent most of my time asking questions like a curious child. "Spring is right around the corner."

"I feel it, too," said Chuck, the talking plant. He often chimed in to agree with me. "Of course, we plants always know about that stuff."

Now, I feel it's my duty here to clarify something about this situation. Chuck is not actually a talking plant. There's no such thing. Chuck is a regular plant.

Kip is insane.

Luckily for everyone, Kip is not the violent, creepy kind of insane. Rather, he is the charming, tragic kind of insane that happens when a sensitive mind is overloaded with the world's brutality. Something snaps and often never heals again.

It's the kind of insane that talks to plants, then tells

everyone else what the plant said back.

Kip certainly had enough opportunity to have been exposed to brutality. He was a veteran of this world's most recent and horrific war. It was one of those game-changing wars, the kind optimists and fools call a war to end all wars.

This world had been a long time coming to its great war. The planet was composed primarily of the lighter elements. Useful metals like iron and copper were rare and valuable; gold and silver were unheard of outside of scientific labs.

Therefore, their technology did not evolve along the customary metallic lines. These people would never achieve the heights of inorganic chemistry and metallurgy that allow for nuclear power or armies of steel juggernauts that tear the land to ribbons.

Unfortunately, that did not spare them the horrors of mass war. Their technology had developed around carbon, silicon, and all of the different configurations that were possible with their unique chemical properties. It had taken their civilization longer to achieve, but they had managed to refine natural fibers and ceramics into materials that would nearly rival the toughest carbon steel.

The latest war had already seen the development of rapid fire projectile weapons, roaring guns that shredded through lines of infantry like invisible demons. Sadly, these weapons only played a minor part in the war's massive casualties. Their real power in technology had derived more from their organic roots: poisons.

These people had developed incredibly advanced biological and chemical weapons. They had managed to engineer compounds, pathogens, and custom viruses that dealt out death with the surety of an artist's brush. Poisons had been used from the very beginning of their culture, so there wasn't the usual shock and horror that often comes when a populace faces such atrocities.

Millions died without even a wound on them. Entire cities were massacred without even one drop of blood to mar the carpets. It was like the old occupants had moved out by choice, leaving a fully functioning city for the victors. No messy bombings.

Of course, as is usually the case, the dead are the lucky ones. It's the survivors that must struggle on with broken bodies and minds in a world that doesn't need them anymore.

Kip was one such survivor. As a veteran, he had survived, endured, participated in, and witnessed countless poison attacks. Some were against the enemy, some were against his own people, and some were against civilian populations who had the bad luck of living in strategically desirable locations.

It's impossible to say whether Kip's mind was wrecked by the things he witnessed and did, or by the inhalation of just enough toxins to burn out his neurons, but not kill him.

This was a common issue concerning veterans, too widespread to investigate and solve, so the government offered "assistance" by letting their damaged veterans stay in free housing, eating government bread. The bare necessities of life were granted freely, in gratitude for their service. The rest of what makes life worth living was left to the veterans themselves.

The place Kip, Chuck, and I shared was a cubic concrete room, one of hundreds in a massive housing edifice that looked exactly like the buildings on either side of it. The plain concrete structures spread themselves over a section of the city like a gray mold. Other patches like this one would be in other places around the city.

As each one represented its own kind of slum, the government had chosen to space them out so as not to create one large area of unstable people that could become a focal point for riots and crime.

While good in theory, it mostly meant there was nowhere in the city a person could go to be far away from the slums.

It was one of my favorite places to live.

For someone without an identity, living among the insane was a breath of fresh air.

I could ask a thousand questions about the world, its history, and its workings, and it would be no stranger than Kip with his talking plant, or Gilda down the hall, who was purportedly visited by aliens every evening as soon as she was alone.

Oddly, these aliens did not seem very interested in world domination or scientific study. Rather, they most often discussed recipes. During the day, she made these recipes. The results could almost be considered proof of alien life, namely, the kind of alien life that enjoys gravel in many of their meals.

Most people avoided Gilda.

Frankly, everybody generally avoided everyone else. While on most worlds, slums gave rise to gangs and the evils that came with them, these slums made out of broken people were much less cohesive. The various states of mental degradation had produced a population of loners.

Of course, that rule had plenty of exceptions. Little pockets of people formed here and there as they found others like them, friends who could understand. Apparently, Kip had found that in me. He hadn't participated in the larger community at all, preferring the company of his plant, Chuck. So I had accepted his invitation to share their little space with great reverence and gratitude. That had been two months ago.

Since that time, nothing at all had happened. We sat and stared at walls, had lively discussions with Chuck about when the weather would change, and did our best to avoid accepting any food from Gilda.

In my eons of wandering, I had often spent long periods of time without any story to observe, but I had usually spent that time walking, driven always by my compulsion to set one foot in front of the other. Only the compelling allure of a story could ever distract me enough to overcome that basic drive.

In this place, however, there didn't seem to be any story going on. I'm sure there had been many during the war, but everything had remained quiet since, as the wounded lands tried to piece together the wreckage they had wrought on each other.

Still, I stayed on. I had an instinct for stories, a deeper sense of great events on the horizon. That instinct blared away in my head like a siren now. It had drawn me to this land, this slum, and even to this apartment. I had never felt a story draw me so powerfully.

And yet, there was no story here.

I had waited two months. Nothing had transpired at all. Nobody arrived, nobody left, and the greater powers of the land stayed quiet. Still, I couldn't bring myself to leave. The instinct that had drawn me here didn't even like to let me leave the apartment, even if there had been somewhere better to go.

I was waiting for something, I just didn't know what.

So now that you understand that Chuck isn't really a

talking plant, I can continue with my story. When Chuck speaks, it is actually Kip telling me what Chuck said. However, in honor of Kip, I refuse to write the entire story with him parroting a plant. So Chuck will retain his own voice for the remainder of my tale.

"You want to get something to eat?" asked Chuck. "I'm starving."

"How can you be starving when all you need is water and light?" Kip shot back.

"Because I'm not getting any water and light, that's why!"

Kip opened his mouth to argue back, but found no holes in Chuck's logic. Instead he turned his attention to me.

"I suppose we could go get something. Do you want anything, Phillip?"

Phillip, in this case, was me. I had been Phillip all week, and it was looking like it might stick. When Kip and I had first met and I suggested that he pick a name for me, he had been positively delighted. However, his excitement about being able to name me had been too much for him, apparently. He had changed his mind many times over the past couple months.

In the space of about eight weeks, I had been called Sam, Curly, Tom, Betty (a confusing time for all involved), Roy, Mathias, Kilak, and a host of others. None of the names had lasted more than a day or two.

Not that this had led to much confusion. Chuck's name was set, as was Kip's, so I knew that any name spoken that wasn't one of these was likely referring to me, as there was never anyone else in the apartment.

"Sure," I responded. "I could go for some cake."

"Cake," in this context, was the slang term for the standard government welfare bread. It was available free for anyone who asked at any of the multiple distribution centers around the city. The government fortified with all the proteins, vitamins, minerals, and calories necessary to sustain life. A man could live on cake and nothing else and show virtually no ill effects.

It also tasted a bit like dried out paper pulp, both dry and dense. The residents in this building occasionally held informal challenges to see who might be able to eat an entire loaf of it without using any water. Usually, these challenges ended with no winners; the stuff simply had to be washed down with water or it wasn't going down at all.

The government had also dyed it red with a cheap food dye that rubbed off in the mouth and left people walking around with red-colored tongues, as if they had just finished a cherry popsicle. The officials had mumbled some sort of rationalization for this, but the real reason was so that only the truly needy would depend on the bread.

In this society, a red mouth was a sign of poverty and shame. The wealthy of the city went to great lengths to make sure no red foods were served at any of their high society parties. It was a simple but effective welfare system, ensuring that none would starve, at least not against their will.

"Are you coming along this time?" Kip asked hopefully. I shook my head apologetically. In the beginning of our friendship, I went along with him on these little errands the few times he left the apartment, and he had been very glad of the company.

Lately, however, the pull had been growing even stronger. The last couple days, I couldn't even bring myself to leave the room. Whatever was going to happen was going to happen any moment.

It had gotten to the point that I even had a fair idea where it was going to happen in the room. There was a spot towards the back corner that had become like a glowing beacon in my mind. I had even gone so far as to rearrange the room to leave the spot clear.

What was going to happen, on the other hand, I had no idea. For the past two months, this had been one of the dullest spots I had ever stayed in, broken up only by occasional arguments between Chuck and Kip about how Chuck's humming kept Kip awake at night.

"How about you, Chuck, you coming?" Kip looked hopefully towards the broad leaves of the stubby plant. He listened for a moment, then brightened. He gathered up the plant and the two of them left the room, leaving me to myself.

I stared expectantly at the spot in the room where the story would commence. I felt like a kid waiting in line for a roller coaster ride. Every instinct in my body screamed at me that the story was starting, right here, right now. However, every sense told me that I was sitting alone in a quiet concrete box on a peaceful planet.

That's when the sound started.

Chapter 2

The currency of dreams and great causes is risk.

-Musings of the Historian

It started out soft, a high-pitched whisper that I felt more than I heard. The sound was oddly familiar, though I couldn't figure out where I had heard it before. It was like one crystal being scraped across another.

Over the next hour, the sound grew louder, emanating from the empty spot in the room. I couldn't see anything making any noise, but now the sound was loud enough to be heard easily. Much louder and it would start being noticeable in the surrounding rooms.

As it grew louder, the tone changed, becoming rougher and more grating. If one could imagine the sound of glass being torn like a sheet of paper, that's what it sounded like--a piercing crystalline distortion.

My spine tingled with excitement and the energy in the room. I couldn't keep the broad smile from my face. Whatever this was, it was going to be big.

Neighbors started to gather around the door, which Kip had left open. Security could be lax when there was nothing worth stealing. As expected, the sound had drawn them like a siren song. Not by its beauty, of course, the sound was terrible to hear. At high volume, it now vibrated right in people's bones and skulls, a

9

resonance of reality.

They held back from actually coming into the room, as if the concrete walls and open door might somehow form a barrier to protect them from whatever otherworldly presence was approaching.

Kip returned just as the air started to bend. He shouldered through the crowd, shouting both his and Chuck's questions, two loaves of cake under one arm and Chuck under the other. No one answered him because there were no answers to be given.

He finally broke through the crush of bystanders to stand in his own room once again. His jaw stood slack and even Chuck was speechless. The air had somehow thickened around the spot where the sound emanated and was now closer in appearance to water.

The thickened air started to swirl in two directions at once. As if on cue, everyone watching blinked and shook their heads, like people seeing an optical illusion. The air swirled both inward and outward at the same time.

It seemed impossible, but it was happening all the same. Suddenly, people found it very hard to watch and many turned away, holding their hands up to their eyes.

I myself was transfixed. Being impossible myself, I couldn't help but feel a little kinship to this anomaly. Anyone who ever looked directly into my eyes often felt similarly disconcerted. The human mind was built to perceive things according to the laws of physics, so anything that didn't match up often caused the mind to skip or lag, like a computer encountering an error in its programming.

For me, it was perfectly clear what was happening. The air was separating from itself; that's why it appeared to be spiraling in both directions at once. Physics generally demanded that when one thing left, another thing would fill its place. That wasn't happening here. The empty spaces were remaining as the air pushed and pulled itself out of the way, forming a two-dimensional gap like a large circle.

Abruptly, the sound stopped and the circle solidified, the edges taking on a solid look and the center filling with images that didn't belong in the apartment.

The images were blurry and obscured, like looking through a broken magnifying glass, but it was clear enough that we were now looking into some other world or reality.

No one watching had any context for such an event, so even the chattering at the doorway was minimal. Some took it as a bad sign and slipped away, likely not stopping until they had left the building entirely.

Most of us remained, staring at the spectacle and waiting to witness whatever would come next. It took nearly half an hour before anything changed.

A shape took form in the circle, growing larger until the images warped around it and it pressed against the barrier. The glass-ripping sound returned for a fraction of a second and then the figure burst through, tripping as it emerged and landing on all fours in the middle of the room.

The face rose. It was a beautiful woman with strong features. Her eyes locked on me, being the closest bystander.

"Take me to your leader."

"You've got to be kidding me," I groaned softly, though not softly enough.

"This is no joke, I assure you," the woman continued. She rose up onto her knees, but remained there, as if begging. "I must talk to whoever or whatever is in charge of this world as soon as possible! Why would I joke about such a thing?!"

"I didn't mean..." I started, but Kip interrupted me.

"What did she say?" His voice held equal measures of horror and awe. I realized at that moment that I had made a mistake. I understood everyone on every world I visited and they had always understood me. Clearly there must have been many different languages, but where I heard them all the same, I had no way of telling them apart.

Obviously this new visitor would be speaking an entirely different language than the many people assembled around her, but only I had understood. Worse, I had already shown that I understood. Nothing for it now, I thought to myself, I'll have to figure out some way of explaining this later.

"She said she requires an audience with the government."

"That's not what I said!" protested the woman.

"Maybe not exactly, but I'm not going to say what you said," I retorted.

"Why not? This is very important, I assure you!"

"I don't doubt it, I just didn't want to say..."

"What's she saying now?" Kip interrupted again.

"She's saying I didn't translate her directly," I explained.

"Well, you didn't," the woman shot in.

"So what did she really say?" Kip pressed.

I sighed, feeling more than a little silly.

"She said, 'take me to your leader.'"

Kip nodded solemnly, approached the woman, and put Chuck down in front of her. He then stood and made a grand sweeping gesture, like a steward introducing a king.

"Dear lady, this is Chuck, our leader. He says he is honored to make your acquaintance."

The woman looked at Chuck, then up at Kip, then to me.

"Why did this man give me a plant? Am I supposed to eat it?" She reached a hand forward, about to rip off a leaf.

"No!" I shouted, maybe a little bit too loudly, as Kip and the woman jumped. Both looked at me expectantly for an explanation.

The absurdity of the situation hit me all at once, and I looked down at my feet, hiding my smile. My whole body shook with the contained laughter. The room was deathly silent, all eyes on me, which only made the situation that much funnier. I laughed until tears ran from my eyes.

I finally managed to rein in my laughter when Kip and the woman both started looking deeply annoyed at my irreverence. However, I had no intention of telling the woman that the plant was being presented as supreme ruler of this world. I also had no intention of letting Kip think that this woman had ripped through time and space to come eat his houseplant.

Only distraction remained.

"What is your name, dear lady?" I asked, bringing the conversation back to where it should have started before it got derailed by cliché demands and houseplant overlords.

"My name is Yrris." she said, finally standing and composing herself. "I am First Lady of Argoth. I volunteered to be first through the Vortex. I'll confess I am a little surprised to be alive."

She said this last with a trace of a relieved smile, the first sign of relaxation from her. Kip sidled over to me and tugged on my sleeve, a silent request for translation.

"Her name is Yrris," I explained.

"Seemed like she said more than that," he accused.

"I gave you the short version," I shrugged. He scowled at me for a moment before turning his attention back to Yrris. He gave her his broadest smile and pointed to his own chest.

"KIP!" he shouted at her. She took a defensive step back at the sudden shout. He repeated the gesture and the shout. She looked at me, threads of panic on her face.

"Have I done something wrong? If I have, please help me make amends. My people need your help desperately."

"You have done nothing wrong, milady." I spoke in soft, soothing tones. "He was merely introducing himself. His name is Kip."

She looked back at him and granted him a careful smile.

"Kip?" she said. He nodded enthusiastically. She then pointed to her own chest, mimicking his motions, "YRRIS!"

I heard a murmur behind me and I remembered the people gathered at the door. It occurred to me that this scene must be quite frightening to them, especially now that people had started shouting. Kip, however, was beaming at his new-found powers of communication.

He pointed at me next.

"PHILLIP!" he shouted. She nodded politely and turned to me to shout her own name, having adapted quickly to this odd custom. I bit my tongue to stop myself from laughing again.

"CHUCK!" he finished, pointing proudly down at the plant. This brought her up short as she was once again confronted with the plant. She looked at me for an explanation, but I was only barely keeping it together.

"The plant's name is Chuck," I offered before I had to go back to biting my tongue. Her eyes stayed on my face a moment longer, trying to discern if maybe this was some sort of bizarre joke. My manic chuckling didn't help.

Finally, she squared her shoulders and shouted her name one more time, this time to the plant.

Once the formalities had been observed, she turned back to her original request.

"Who leads this world?" she asked me.

"There's a parliamentary form of government with two primary branches," I explained to her, drawing on my very limited knowledge of the local leadership. "So there's not just one leader, though I suppose the Minister would probably have the most pull. In truth, this world itself is not fully united, there are different factions who war against each other."

She looked especially distraught about this last tidbit of news.

"Then who would I talk to about helping us?" Despair laced her voice and it was more a plea for help than a true request for information.

"I wouldn't worry too much about that, milady. Someone will be in touch with us shortly."

"How do you know that? Have you signaled someone?"

"There's no need. Human nature will take care of notifying the right people. By now, the scared people in the hallway will have contacted the local constable. He will be here momentarily."

"And I will talk to him?"

"Heavens no. Chances are, we won't even see him. He will only come as far as is necessary to verify the stories he's been told. He will then decide that it's too much trouble for him and he will dash to tell his supervisor."

"And I will talk to the supervisor?" she pressed, anxious for an answer. While I sensed she was in a hurry, I knew full well that there was no way to hurry the process, so I took my time explaining.

"I'm afraid not. The supervisor will follow the exact same course as the constable and come to the same conclusion. The pattern will repeat itself many times over as the message of your arrival moves up the chain of command."

"Until it reaches the leader?" she asked hopefully. I shook my head again.

"Until it reaches someone willing to take ownership of the situation. It might not be the leader of the nation here, but it will be someone with power and a burning ambition to acquire more."

She looked fully unnerved at my explanation. Her eyes even darted back towards the portal for a moment, checking her escape route.

"Someone like that would be a very dangerous person, yes?"

I smiled and leaned forward, meeting her gaze. She averted her eyes from meeting mine, but I knew I had her full attention.

"Yes, it will be a very dangerous person indeed who comes to talk to you. But then, that's exactly what you came looking for, wasn't it?"

Chapter 3

The line between technology and magic is a thin one.
-Musings of the Historian

Her eyes flashed back to mine and narrowed. The suspicious look passed immediately, but a cold curiosity remained.

"Maybe I am talking to a dangerous man right now," she said softly.

"Maybe," I agreed. "But not in this story. I am no danger to you or your enemies."

"*Hmph,*" she grunted. Either she did not believe me, or she was a bit disappointed. It was hard to tell.

"Okay, what has she said so far?" Kip was back in the conversation now. He had been busying himself around the apartment as if making it appropriate for company. Some sort of ribbon was pinned on his shirt. On a uniform, it likely would have looked impressive. On his shirt, it looked more like something that had landed there by mistake and needed to be brushed off. Still, he puffed his chest out proudly as he rejoined our little group.

From out in the hallway, I heard new footsteps and a whispered conference. The constable had shown up. I glanced out in the hallway and could already see the crisp uniform retreating hastily back the way he had come. The supervisor would know what was happening very soon.

If the constable had a solid reputation, this would go a lot faster. If not, the supervisor would insist on coming to check the situation himself before passing it up the line.

Luck must have been with us, because we never saw the supervisor or any other middlemen. It took only about half an hour before a real commotion started.

Slate gray uniforms filled the hall like a smoke grenade. Soldiers pointed weapons and shouted. The people still crowded in the hallway were quickly and efficiently rounded up and herded away like cattle, undoubtedly to be quarantined, questioned, and tested.

Yrris stood up, worry on her face. Kip moved between her and the door protectively. I motioned them both to sit back down.

"This is only the lightning, a bright flash. Wait for the thunder."

Both of them sat back down, but neither of them looked comforted as we watched the building locked down under military control. The room itself was left entirely alone. A few soldiers dared to glance in, but even they looked away as if stung.

I guessed that their orders were to not pay any attention to the room at all. The fact that they looked so guilty when their discipline slipped told me that the orders were given by someone they feared.

A dangerous man.

Finally, the hallways were cleared of civilians and most of the soldiers left as well, only a couple remaining behind as guards.

Then the door at the end of the hallway opened and new footsteps approached down the corridor. These new steps weren't hurried; they had the steady cadence of a military march. When they rounded the corner and we could see the party, I was surprised at how young the man was. I had expected someone with more gray in his hair, but this man was likely still in his thirties.

He was flanked by two attendants, a man and a woman who looked to their leader occasionally as if trying to read his thoughts, anticipate his needs.

They took the room in with a single glance. Not that it was much of a task. Even taking into account the bizarre portal in the corner, it was still a very small and plain room. The male attendant produced a folding chair and set it down for the man in the middle. He declined to sit, however.

"I am Colonel Daws," he stated, addressing himself directly to our new visitor. While still human, she certainly had a different look about her than the local populace.

Her head was a little wider at the forehead and slimmer at the chin, giving her face the appearance of a triangle pointing down. The effect was not pronounced or unpleasant, however. She was still quite pretty.

Yrris looked to me for a translation.

"He says his name is Colonel Daws."

She nodded and stood. She pointed to her chest and I smiled.

"YRRIS!" she yelled. The two attendants started at the sudden outburst, as if they had been expecting an attack. The Colonel was unmoved. In fact, he hadn't seemed to notice at all. As soon as I had repeated what he had said to her, his eyes had locked on me like a cat eyeing a mouse.

"Why repeat what I said?" he asked me.

"So the Lady Yrris could understand." I bobbed my head submissively, keeping my eyes down.

"But you didn't say anything different," he pointed out.

"So it would seem, Colonel."

"So she understands our language?"

"No, Colonel."

"But she understands you." His eyes continued to bore into me, suspicion furrowing his brow.

"Yes, Colonel," I bobbed my head again.

"Why?" The word was loaded with equal measures of curiosity and accusation.

"I don't know! I was just waiting here for Kip and Chuck to get back with cake, and then Chuck started going off about how Kip doesn't get him enough sun..." I rambled off an incoherent narrative and Daws cut me off again.

"Where is Chuck?" The attendants were already combing through papers they produced from legal looking cases. Most likely the papers were a catalogue of the tenants that had been taken away.

"He's right there," I pointed down to the plant at Yrris's feet.

"Pleasure to meet you," said Chuck.

The Colonel's narrowed eyes now turned on Kip, who had of course supplied the voice to Chuck's friendly salutation.

"And I'm Kip," Kip offered.

The female attendant found a paper and held it up for the Colonel. He scanned it briefly and turned back to Kip.

"Pleasure to meet you and Chuck, Kip. Thank you for letting us use your apartment." The Colonel's military stiffness faded in a second and he was all charm. Kip smiled broadly at the Colonel's friendly manner.

"Of course! Anything to help," Kip answered.

"You can count on us," Chuck added.

"And what is your name?" Daws turned his attention back to me.

20

"I can't remember," I shrugged. "I think somebody took it away from me."

Kip nodded enthusiastically. "We call him Phillip, but you can change it if you want to, he doesn't mind."

"Phillip is fine. Nice to meet you, Phillip." Daws inclined his head in a slight bow, though I didn't miss the added suspicion in his eyes. It wasn't over between Daws and me, but he was picking his battles.

"Could you please tell Lady Yrris that we are happy that she has chosen to visit us? Then please ask her why she has chosen to come here."

I could feel Daws's frustration as I seemingly repeated back the same words in the same language to Yrris. Still, she lit up once I was done and struck right at the heart of the matter.

"My people need help and your people need to be warned, so I have come through the Vortex as an ambassador from my people."

When I had translated this for Colonel Daws, he breathed deeply to the sound of his two attendants scribbling away rapidly on fresh sheets of paper behind him.

"What is the danger you face?" he asked through me.

"Our world is ruled by the Tanniks." Her eyes flicked nervously to the Vortex behind her as she said the name. Daws caught the meaning behind the glance even before I had finished translating. A whispered command sent the male attendant out the door and running down the hall.

Unless I had greatly underestimated the Colonel, the building would be surrounded by their heaviest weaponry within the hour, if it wasn't already.

"The Vortex is the source of their power, though we have

never seen it open like this. They use this power to enslave us all; we are a world of cattle."

Kip laid a hand on her shoulder in solidarity as I translated this newest bit of information. I'm sure the thought of her being enslaved made him quite sad. The Colonel, however, had drawn entirely different conclusions from the same story.

"What is this power they are drawing from our world?"

"They use it to fuel their magic."

The Colonel scowled at me again when I translated this, thinking that I was messing with the translation. Still, it wasn't the time to argue with the only translator he had, even if he didn't understand how parroting back his words counted as translating.

"What kind of magic do they possess?" he asked, trying to work his way around my mistranslation to get a description of whatever technology these aliens used.

"Each Tannik specializes in its own type of magic. Most of them dominate through pure elemental force, but there are those whose powers are simply beyond description."

The Colonel waved this aside with a shake of his head. Her subjective views on the Tanniks' power didn't give him any useable intelligence.

"Could you give me an example of their magic?" he asked instead, trying again for some objective view of the threat.

Yrris shrugged once she understood his request.

"I can't give any example that would be close to their power, but I suppose it would look similar to this."

I never got a chance to translate what she said, because even as she said it, she put her hands out in front of her and turned them palms up. Instantly, the air rushed upward through her hands like a wind tunnel.

22

The female attendant staggered backwards and Kip tripped over his chair. Only the Colonel and I leaned forward to get a closer look at the display.

Once she had the momentum going, she focused the air currents into a tight spiral that barely disturbed the air in the rest of the apartment. She used the pressures to lift Chuck off the ground, buoying him up with the rapidly cycling air.

She then gently lowered him to the ground, letting the air currents weaken in intensity until Chuck's pot clattered softly to rest on the concrete. She turned her hands back down and shrugged again.

"As I said, it's not much. Shawen, the Air Tannik, could rip a mountain from its roots."

Chapter 4

More than half of good decision making consists of choosing the right people to trust.

–Musings of the Historian

For the first time, the Colonel looked impressed as I translated this last bit. He looked towards the Vortex with new interest.

"Are they intelligent?" he asked. This time, it was my turn to narrow my eyes at him. There were undertones to that question that the rest of the people in the room wouldn't understand. This Daws would take some watching.

"Oh yes. They are very intelligent."

"Can they be reasoned with?" I really didn't like where his mind was going, but I translated it anyway. Yrris shook her head vigorously.

"They do not speak with people. They see us like insects, far below them. I don't think they even need us; it's some sort of sick little game for them to torment us."

The lights behind the Colonel's eyes were working like a supercomputer, calculating angles and advantages. This was a man who saw gods only in himself. Even the Tanniks would only be pawns in his mind. I wondered if Yrris had any notion of what forces she had put into motion.

"Will they be coming here through that portal?" he asked, motioning to the Vortex.

24

"I don't think so," she replied. "Most of them are too big to fit through a Vortex of this size; they would have to make a much bigger one. Also, there is the question of whether or not their magic would work in this world."

The Colonel's eyes narrowed ever so slightly at this latest bit of information.

"I suppose they know now," he stated flatly. The female attendant behind him moved meaningfully to stand between Yrris and the Vortex. Yrris watched her wide-eyed as I translated what the Colonel had said.

"I don't understand."

"The Colonel thinks you might be a spy, like a test subject sent ahead of an invasion to check if the magic would work here," I filled in for her. "So the young lady here just became a guard. If you try to pass back through the portal, she will kill you."

"What?!" Both Yrris and Daws shouted the word at once, sounding in unison to my ears, though they undoubtedly sounded different to each other. Yrris was deeply offended at suddenly being a prisoner, and the Colonel was offended at having his motives relayed so openly to a possible enemy.

Even Chuck looked a little miffed.

I shrugged to them all.

"Hey, I'm the translator here and I'm going to translate everything. You don't like it, get someone else!"

I folded my arms and *hmphed* like a pouting child. Yrris put her hand on my forearm to comfort me. The motion made me jump a bit and I took her hand off of my forearm and placed it on my shoulder instead.

"That spot is taken, my Lady," I offered as explanation, though she only looked more confused. "But I thank you for the gesture."

"Well isn't that cozy?" the Colonel remarked, looking at the hand on my shoulder. "She understands you, but no one else, and now you're acting like you're old friends. We also have no record of you living here. Am I really supposed to believe you only met today? At this point, the only one above suspicion here is the bloody plant!"

"It's not like it's my fault!" I protested. "It's not like she's telling you everything either."

"Like what?" he demanded. Out of the corner of my eye, Yrris was shooting me an outraged look. Her hand left my shoulder.

"Like how many more people are going to be coming through that Vortex."

"Did she tell you that?"

"She hardly had to tell me, Colonel. She's miffed that you don't trust her, but she obviously isn't that upset about being blocked from the Vortex. That means that either she has another way back, which is unlikely, or she wasn't intending on going back anyway, which would suggest that she was planning on having her people come here."

Both Yrris and Daws stared at me, then at each other. Daws kept his eyes on Yrris, but asked me:

"How did you figure all that out so quickly?"

I pointed to Kip, who looked panicked and immediately pointed at Chuck. Chuck pointed at no one, but Daws didn't seem to care.

The first signs of frustration were starting to seep into his face. He looked to his female attendant, who stood at full attention between Yrris and the Vortex.

"Lori, give me your analysis of the room," he ordered.

All eyes turned to the young woman. She had blond hair pulled up into a bun so tight it made her face look slightly stretched, as if it had been freshly ironed. The rest of her appearance followed suit. Her uniform was immaculately pressed and fit tightly. Everything about her spoke of military precision. Even the planes of her face were set in firm, straight lines.

I hadn't paid her much attention when she first entered the room; she had been a mere appendage to Colonel Daws. However, now that I knew the Colonel a little better, I realized that a man like that would have no interest in fawning sycophants.

The two people walking at his right and left hand would be there because they brought something valuable, or powerful, to the game. The young lady proved my suspicions correct as she talked her way around the room.

"Yes, Colonel." She nodded smartly and launched into her observations, including intricate detail, though she never once glanced towards any notes. "The room is registered to Kipland Talex, the man to your far left.

"His record and the ribbon on his chest place him as a veteran of at least three major actions during the war. During these actions, there were possibilities that he was exposed to Solanis compounds C, F, and G and the Gury gas. Both the Gury gas and Solanis G have been shown to cause brain damage and psychosis when received in trace amounts.

"The man living with him is an unknown, though that is not uncommon in these sectors. He shows similar symptoms to Mr. Talex…"

"Please, call me Kip." Mr. Talex interrupted. She nodded again and continued.

27

"His lack of a name could possibly be attributed to exposure to Haxis A, a compound used only in the very latest stages of the war and known to cause dissociative disorders."

"Do you know why he would be understood by everyone?" Daws asked.

"No, Colonel."

"Then theorize."

"Yes, Colonel. We have established that he was the only one in the room at the time of the anomaly. The neighbors said no one else entered the room until almost the very end of the event. I theorize that whatever power opened the portal also provided for a means of communication."

"It taught him their language by opening?" the Colonel asked, not incredulously, just clarifying.

"No, Colonel. The fact that we hear no other language from him suggests that the link is mental. Both we and the Lady Yrris are hearing meaning, the words themselves are only perceived, filled in by our own minds."

"So it's possible that he's actually speaking their language instead of ours?" Daws asked, leaning forward, truly fascinated. I was leaning forward myself, though towards Lori, eyes wide in genuine amazement.

This was the closest anyone had ever gotten to the truth of the matter in all my wanderings. Further, she had concluded all of this within minutes of meeting me. This woman Lori was both brilliant and intuitive. One to watch...

"It's possible, of course, Colonel. But it is even more likely that he is speaking neither language. It's even possible that he's speaking no language at all at this point."

"Fascinating," he replied, his eyes fixed on me again.

"Would there be any benefit to studying him?"

"Possibly, but it is more likely that the ability is tied to the Vortex anomaly, not any sort of physiological alteration in him. I would suggest that he not be allowed to leave the room, just in case we lose the connection and the ability to communicate."

Daws nodded and I mentally settled in for the long haul. I would have a front row seat for the show, but I'd be chained to it.

"Very well, I am making his safety your personal responsibility. Do you think he can be trusted?"

"I don't know, Colonel."

"Then theorize."

"Then yes, I feel he can be trusted."

Daws waited a moment, expecting more from her. When nothing came he prompted:

"What is that theory based on?"

"A feeling, Colonel," she confessed, looking a little sheepish. "I'm sorry."

"No, it's okay. I feel it, too, but it doesn't make sense. What about this magic she has?"

"There's still a lot there I don't understand, but she's said that it's based around this anomaly. A connection between our two worlds would naturally lead to an imbalance, and imbalances can be used to generate energy."

"Like a dam?" Daws asked. "The water is higher on one side and we run generators off the contained energy of the reservoir?"

"That's actually a perfect example, sir," Lori said, clearly impressed. "There's no way our two worlds could be the same in every aspect, so there must be a flow of some kind."

"I can see that," Daws mused. "But a flow of what? And why would their magic work on this side? You would lose your energy if you tried moving to the upper reservoir, wouldn't you?"

Lori was already shaking her head. "The pure imbalance is only the fuel, not the engine. Once the water flows through a generator, we don't need the water anymore. We can transmit the electric current through the polymer network to wherever we want."

"So if we figured out how to close the Vortex...?"

"The magic would cease. Without fuel, the engine stops," Lori confirmed. "Though I don't think we have much hope of that, sir. Our scientists have theorized about dimensional physics, but that's as far as that field has gone. So I can only think this is something wrought by their magic."

Daws accepted her explanation and moved on.

"What about the Lady Yrris?"

Yrris perked up at her name. She had been taking the time to study the room herself, but she interrupted now.

"What have they been talking about?" she asked me.

"Well, Daws here felt the situation getting too weird for him, so he sought the advice of someone smarter than him."

Daws's eyes narrowed ever so slightly at me, and I thought I saw the shadow of a smile flick across Lori's face before it was thoroughly buried under martial discipline.

"And the girl is smarter than him?" Yrris queried, looking at Lori with new interest. I nodded. "Then shouldn't we be talking to her instead of Daws?"

"Oh no," I lectured. "Intelligence is only one form of power. A cannon might be the most powerful piece in the army, but you don't let the cannon lead the troops. Daws is the general and he wields Lori's intelligence like he would wield any other power."

This time it was Lori's eyes that narrowed at me and Daws's

face that showed a flicker of amusement. Yrris still looked confused.

"I thought you said he was a colonel, not a general."

"He's only a colonel because that's what serves him best right now. Rank is a tool like any other."

"You can't tell me that's natural," Daws protested to Lori. "Are we really supposed to believe that a crazy person rotting in the slums is capable of these advanced insights?"

"Actually, Colonel, it's not only possible, it may explain a few things. If he were a member of military intelligence, that might help explain his lack of identity, as well as his knack for analyzing people.

"Chemical damage to his brain wouldn't necessarily damage his analytic abilities. Most likely, it damaged the part of his mind that manages inhibitions and judgment, which would clarify why he speaks whatever he's thinking and why he so easily fell into the same delusions as Kip."

"What the devil is she talking about, delusions?!" asked Chuck the talking plant. No one answered him.

"Very well, so let's get back to where we were interrupted. Continue your analysis. What can you tell me about our new visitor?"

Lori launched back into her briefing, her eyes now on Yrris.

"She is someone of great importance, used to having attention paid to her. She is clearly very brave and even more desperate. Whatever danger her people are facing, she considered it worth her life. She's confident in her own abilities and has trouble trusting others with anything of importance."

"Very well." The Colonel's mind locked all of this new information away. He seemed to sit a little straighter as he felt control returning with the new knowledge.

"And the plant?" he asked. I couldn't tell if he was joking or not, his face was as serious as ever. Lori responded in kind, thorough and efficient.

"A common houseplant when kept in small pots, as this one is, to limit its size. When in fields or in the wild, it grows into a medium sized tree that produces a largely tasteless fruit that is still very nutritious and used in making bread favored by those in the southern territories.

"This one shows no peculiar characteristics…or intelligence, at the present time. It appears to be in moderately good health. It could use some more sun."

Chapter 5

Whether it's people, animals, or machines, control is all about finding the right pressure points. The more that is understood about guiding forces and motivations, the more possibilities unfold.

–Musings of the Historian

"Well then, it appears that I've got all the information I need, doesn't it?" Daws drawled, the casual tone sounding a little strange coming from him, like an actor switching characters. I could see the gears turning behind his eyes. "Perhaps it's time we educate everyone else a little."

He drew his sidearm. It was a bulky thing. It lacked the sleek look of pistols and blasters I had seen on worlds that had more metals. Still, it was built for function, not looks, and I had no doubt it was plenty dangerous. And if any of us had any doubts in that regard, Daws himself soon dispelled them as he narrated the gun's abilities.

"Do you all see this cylinder here? It holds an explosive gas that our chemists are incredibly proud of. It only takes an injection of a very small amount into the firing chamber here to shoot a fiber pellet through three inches of concrete."

He paused, politely gesturing to Yrris, indicating that I should translate for her. I did so grudgingly, uncomfortable with his heavy-handed threats. But he wasn't done yet.

"This single cylinder is enough to fire over two hundred

fiber-weave pellets before needing to be replaced. I imagine our friend Kip here saw similar models during the war, didn't you, Kip? Though they were likely the two-canister models."

Kip nodded, his eyes fixed on the weapon as he subconsciously slouched, cringing inwardly away from the weapon.

"But this one isn't exactly like the army issue firearms," Daws continued, turning the weapon over to show us a switch on the barrel. "No, this is a prototype model for the next production line of weapons. It has a feature that allows me to use the gas more directly. If I flip this switch…"

Daws dramatically flipped the switch, making sure everyone in the room saw it.

"Then no pellet is loaded in the firing chamber and the gas flows freely after ignition, shooting out of the barrel all at once in a devastating spray of flame. I hear it can incinerate anything within ten feet. Would you like to see?"

The barrel was pointed leisurely at no one in particular, resting on his lap where he had been displaying it. No one said anything, but Kip shook his head slightly. Daws laughed, a cold sound.

"Don't everybody look so serious. It's not like I'm going to fry one of you for a demonstration. A plant, however…"

He snatched the gun up and pointed it directly at Chuck, the talking plant.

"No!" Kip yelped, throwing himself forward as if to jump in front of the gun, though he was too far away to have made it regardless.

Daws wasn't looking at Kip, however; he was looking at me. He met my eyes and smiled, a subtle nod as he confirmed his suspicions.

He had fooled me. The show had been a test and I had missed it. I had been acting as crazy as Kip, talking to Chuck and letting random nonsense guide my conversation. Then Chuck had been in danger. Kip, who truly saw Chuck as a companion and friend, had been frightened and concerned, as anyone would be. I, however, had been distracted by Daws himself.

I had thought that the show of force was a bully throwing his weight around, asserting his authority over those who couldn't fight back. I realized too late that he had been testing me and Kip, seeing if we really believed our own insane ramblings.

It was a small thing--he had already suspected me--but it was a galling defeat, nonetheless. I, a Historian with hundreds of years of practiced deception, had had my cover story dismantled within minutes. I decided right then and there I didn't like Colonel Daws. I was surprised at the emotion, as it was petty and jealous, but there it was all the same.

Worse, he wasn't done. Kip had pulled himself up short. After the initial rush, he realized that he was about to put himself in the line of fire. As much as he loved Chuck, he stopped and instead turned to begging.

"Please don't kill him! He hasn't hurt anyone."

"Yes," Chuck chimed in. "I can't even hurt anyone. I'm a plant!"

Daws's hand stayed steady, the barrel aimed at point blank range at the helpless plant.

"I don't want to hurt anyone, especially not a nice plant like Chuck here." The Colonel's voice was calm and soothing now, and Kip responded to it, daring to relax a little, though Chuck's life still hung on the pull of a trigger.

"The thing is, I wanted to learn something. I could learn something about my weapon, but that would mean hurting Chuck here. Maybe there's something else I could learn?"

"We'll tell you anything!" yelped Chuck. Kip's eyes, however, narrowed with suspicion.

"What would you like to learn instead?"

"So glad you asked." Daws reminded me in that moment of a snake, calm and satisfied that his prey could not escape. "As curious as I am about how this weapon would work, I'm even more curious about how things look on the other side of that portal. Would you mind taking a look for me?"

Kip paled a little, but he looked toward the portal meaningfully.

"No, Kip, you can't!" I blubbered, waving my hands at him. "There's no way to know what's on the other side. Who knows what might happen to you? He's using you as bait!"

My frightened ramblings only seemed to steel Kip. Knowing that it was dangerous made it seem worth something in the weary veteran's mind. Surely if he did a dangerous thing for the man in charge, that would be worth Chuck's life.

He stepped toward the Vortex. I let him step past me, then I was up on my feet, behind his elbow, pleading with him not to go. My voice broke with fear and my feet dragged along the floor as if my very body was rebelling at the idea of going near the portal.

Kip continued, resolute, past where Lori stood guard between Yrris and the Vortex. Only a step or two remained. I made three quick steps, almost like a dance. Left, right, left, and I was standing in front of Kip and in front of the portal.

I made eye contact with Daws, winked, and stepped backward through the Vortex.

It would be easy for me, as the storyteller, to pass off what I did as a necessary maneuver to witness another part of the story.

After all, Daws had made it perfectly clear that he wouldn't risk me. I was his only translator, which meant there was never any chance of me being put in a dangerous situation. Naturally, if I was going to see the other side of the Vortex, I needed to trick him.

Yes, I could make that claim. Sadly, I would be lying. The fact was that I was still feeling stung by him getting a step ahead of me. There was a part of me that rankled at the thought of this cunning Colonel outwitting me, even if it was a small thing. I took a childish joy in outsmarting him and getting myself on the far side of the portal.

Even in the moment of my little triumph, seeing the Colonel's eyes widen as he realized I'd played him, I still braced myself as I hit the portal. I didn't know what to expect, or if the portal would even work for a being like myself. I had never seen such a thing, so all the rules were unknown. My stomach clenched as I felt myself pass through.

Sure enough, what I experienced was nothing I could have expected.

It was familiar.

Chapter 6

When in a new situation, seek first to understand before you try to affect any change.

                              -Musings of the Historian

There was no burst of cold or buzzing as my molecules were scattered and rearranged. The horizons shifted. It was the same thing I had felt hundreds of times before in my wanderings.

The implications staggered me. For the first few seconds, I didn't even register all the people around me, some pressing forward toward me, and some staggering back in surprise.

This is what happened to me. I never saw any portal, the air never spiraled away from itself, but the feeling was undeniably the same. I had discovered the mechanism by which I traveled between worlds.

The problem was, I wasn't the one controlling where and when the shifts happened. I had always accepted this as a basic fact of my existence, but now I was standing on the far end of a portal, feeling the same sensation of shifting horizons, and it was man-made.

I didn't get much time to muse over this new revelation, however. I had stepped into the middle of a frantic crowd of people. The more nervous segment of them, seeing a stranger, had already started their retreat, stumbling over each other as they put distance between themselves and me. Other braver souls were doing the exact opposite. They pressed forward and seemed ready to maul me.

One of the men took control, even going so far as to put his hand on my shoulder.

"Who are you? What happened to Lady Yrris?" he asked. The man overflowed with desperate urgency. Something struck me as odd about the situation immediately, though I couldn't put my finger on exactly what was wrong.

"I'm a tourist," I commented, though the word didn't seem to register any meaning in his mind at all. "Lady Yrris is fine, she's getting to know the locals on the other side."

"How can that be?" His confusion confused me. Concern or even fear was perfectly understandable. Their leader had just stepped through a bizarre anomaly. However, the complete bewilderment he was showing was odd.

"It's not that hard, people are pretty friendly, most places you go," I said, avoiding real answers while I studied my surroundings.

At first I thought that we might be in some sort of vast cave, with cooking fires providing a little light to see the roof of the cavern. But after a moment's focus, I realized that we were actually outside.

The sky was a deep, splotchy red. Dark streaks riddled the sky like stringy clouds at twilight. But I hadn't seen clouds take such shapes before, and I considered myself something of an expert on cloud formations. There was some darker pollution at work here than mere water vapor.

"Did you speak with her, then?" the man pressed, drawing my attention back to the conversation.

"Oh yes," I responded. "We're old friends now."

The confusion only grew in his eyes, but he pushed on like

a good soldier.

"Should we follow, then? Is it safe? Death is almost here!"

"Something's going to kill you?" I asked, looking over the landscape again, trying to locate the threat that had these people so panicked.

"Yes, Lady Yrris said we should follow when he got close. Our lookouts say he's still about an hour away, but if it's not safe, we should get clear of this area before he gets here. It will take us some time."

"He? Who's coming?"

The man quivered with fear and frustration now, trying to get me to understand.

"Death! He's on his way."

"Death is a Tannik come to wipe you out, correct?"

He nodded. The people looked even more nervous at the discussion of their approaching doom. Still, they looked to me. Or rather, they were looking to Lady Yrris through me. These were not brave people. Even the boldest among them were begging for instruction. Yrris had given them courage somehow. Now they needed her to tell them to be brave again. That's why they looked at me with such wide eyes.

I was still missing something.

"You're an army," I observed. They didn't have uniforms and they didn't look fit to fight the way they were cringing and cowering, but the group was made up entirely of able-bodied men and women, no young or old among them.

The man laughed at my assessment, though it was a bitter sound, lacking any real amusement.

"Our settlement was going to be punished. We traveled here to make our stand. Our magic is strongest near the Vortex. When the portal opened, it was like a miracle. Yrris ran right through, saying we should follow when Death got close."

Another ping in my mind. Something didn't fit. The temporary leader practically growled with frustration and impatience as I methodically thought through the situation.

"So Death was coming to wipe out your village for some little act of rebellion. You took your best people and headed this way for a showdown, drawing Death away from your children and elderly.

"Once you got here, the Vortex opened and Yrris dashed through first, right away, to test it and try to find a place to hide on the far side. Is that all correct?"

Another nod. That was it. Now the question to bring it all together.

"How long ago was that?" I asked, feeling a little smug at having put the puzzle together.

"A couple minutes," he responded and I had my solution confirmed.

It was time to get back. First I needed to deal with this crowd.

"What will Death do when he gets here?" I prompted, loading my tone with suggestion, as if the orders should be obvious.

"He will consume everything within miles of this place. He…"

"And then?" I interrupted. He blanched as he realized the only possible eventuality.

"He will go through the Vortex to destroy everything beyond."

"I'm certain Lady Yrris would want you to be safe."

The man nodded and started shouting orders. To their credit, once they had direction, the people moved with incredible efficiency, gathering their supplies and scattering. They would flee this place until they were well out of the way of suspicion.

I felt no conflict or inner pain. I hadn't actually influenced the story. They would have made the same decision in ten minutes, whether I had shown up or not, once they'd thought through the situation.

They had been so eager to leave that none had even stopped to consider that I hadn't really said much of anything at all. I had conveyed no orders. But it had been enough. They filled in the blanks in their minds.

I stood and watched them for a minute or two, giving Daws a little more time to sweat. I took a moment to observe these people. Beyond the fact that they were clearly terrified, their clothes suggested heavy wear and continual use. Their frightened movements still showed the strength and steady endurance of people used to long labor. These people were slaves.

Obviously, none of them were available to answer any of my questions at the moment, and there wasn't much more I could learn from distant observation. I gave them a good-hearted wave and walked back through the Vortex.

I nearly ran into a group of soldiers, dressed in full battle gear and ready for anything. Every weapon was trained on me.

"Hold!" Daws commanded, then directed the soldiers to take up positions back in the hallway. Kip was cowering in his chair, clutching Chuck close to him.

"I expect a thorough report, Phillip," Daws fumed, once the soldiers had closed the door behind them. "You certainly took your time getting back. We were about to come in after you."

"I'm touched." I smiled at him, though I was certain his concern hadn't been for my well-being. He waited for his report, but I turned first to Lady Yrris.

"Your people have decided to hide until Death has passed through the Vortex."

She breathed a sigh of relief to hear that her people were out of harm's way. Daws forcibly reinserted himself into the conversation.

"What do you mean? What's coming through?" he demanded. "And if there was an active threat, why did you take so long getting back here?"

"Ah yes, that's the key thing in all this, Colonel. Time is running slower on their world."

Silence filled the room as everyone tried to digest this new information.

"You're going to have to run that by me again," Chuck quipped. Daws rolled his eyes at Kip, but then nodded and looked back at me.

"As bizarre as this sounds, I'm going to have to agree with the blasted plant! Do explain yourself, Phillip. What is this about time running differently? And how is that the key to all this? Doesn't the approach of this Death character seem a bit more urgent?"

"I'm sure Lady Yrris can tell us all about Death. The key thing is that it means you have time to prepare. The Vortex links these two worlds, but that doesn't make the same laws apply for each world. On this world, time is running faster than it is on that one."

"You mean our world, right?" Kip interrupted.

"What?"

"You said, 'this world.' You mean 'our world,' don't you?"

"Of course, Kip. Our world." I comforted him, but I was feeling my cover story start to unravel as even kind, trusting Kip was seeing little slips in my speech. I moved to divert everyone's attention back to the story, where it should be.

"The point is that while an hour passes on their world, over half a day is passing on our world."

"That can't be possible," Lori protested. Her finely tuned analytical mind was having trouble processing such a large break from what she knew to be true. "Time is just a construct, a way of establishing sequence. How can things be happening faster there?"

"That all becomes clear when you realize that you're wrong, my dear Lori." She bristled, both at my patronizing tone and the insinuation that she was wrong. To her credit, she kept listening. "Time is not just a human concept. It is a dimension of reality with rules that govern it like any other. So time will work according to the same rules there as here, but there's nothing stopping it from running at a different rate.

"Think of it like a rotating disc. Near the center of the disc, things will be moving very slowly. On the outside of the disc, it's moving very fast. It's the same disc, but capable of existing at different speeds simultaneously. It's over-simplified, but you can think of us as existing near the edge of the disc. Yrris' world exists more towards the center. So, a big move in our time translates to a much smaller move in their time. All clear?"

Lori stared at me for a long moment before turning to Daws.

"Colonel, I retract my earlier analysis of this man. I no longer believe that he was a member of military intelligence. I am also reconsidering my earlier feeling that he can be trusted."

There went the last shreds of my cover story. It seemed that the only one left in the room who saw me as a simple player in all this was Chuck, the talking plant, and I imagined to myself that his leaves were hanging in a suspicious manner.

"I agree, Lori," Daws began. "Do not let him through the Vortex again. Now, I need to know more about what this means for us. Phillip, I must insist that you finish your report. I'll accept that time is moving faster on this side, for now. What does that mean for us here?"

"You know, it's much more fun when you figure it out for yourself," I chided. "But I suppose we might as well cut to the chase. The people on the other side said that Death was coming in under an hour. I saw enough fear in their eyes to convince me that whoever this is, he is a terrifying enemy. Luckily, an hour on their side is going to be many long hours for us here.

"You can learn all you can about your enemy from Lady Yrris here and make your preparations accordingly. It's like playing against someone who has to move in slow motion."

Daws's eyes lit up as he put the pieces together in his mind. He turned to Lady Yrris with a greedy, wolfish smile.

"What do you know about Death?"

Chapter 7

Even absolute truths can look relative when skewed by skillful presentation.

-Musings of the Historian

Lady Yrris had already seen the question coming and didn't wait for me to translate.

"Death is a swarm Tannik. We call him Death because he claims all dead bodies, consuming them to replenish and to grow. We've never seen him eat any sort of vegetation, and he only seems interested in the larger animal species. Humans appear to be his preferred food."

Bitterness crept into Yrris' voice as she shared this last tidbit. I translated everything word for word to Daws, who seemed remarkably unimpressed by these revelations. He went right into his follow-up questions.

"Explain more of what you meant by 'swarm Tannik,'" he prompted. I passed the query along.

"He doesn't have a regular body like you and me. He is made up of small, flying parts, like wasps. Every tiny piece can see, hear, and even speak in its own way, but all are governed by some sort of central mind that we've never been able to understand.

"He is usually the first to respond to any sort of rebellion or threat. He can sneak into the smallest cracks, overhear whispered conversations, and root out any kind of defiance. Then he can

46

descend on the perpetrators and grind them into nothing one tiny bite at a time. It's a horrifying thing to watch, a message to anyone else who would threaten him or the Tannik rule."

Daws absorbed all of this information stoically. He went to the wall and plugged in his communicator.

As I mentioned before, this planet hadn't been blessed with an abundance of many of the heavier metals. They had some copper, but it was rare enough that they couldn't use it for electrical infrastructure.

Instead, they had developed a fascinating liquid polymer that was highly conductive. It wasn't as conductive as the copper or even gold that other planets used, but it had the benefit of being incredibly cheap to produce.

They had an amazing network of this stuff that they had running through every room of every building. The supply was constantly being circulated by massive central pumps in every city.

It was the basis of many of their other technologies. During their cold winters, the same polymer could be run over catalysts that made it heat up, providing a heating system for every space with no substantial extra cost.

Best of all, the polymer was particularly adept at transmitting radio frequencies, even multiple frequencies on the same line. So any government official could plug in and connect to anyone else anywhere on the network.

Now the Colonel used this network to jump from conversation to conversation. There were no pleasantries nor introductions. Every person he phoned was clearly expecting the call. More of my suspicions were confirmed about Colonel Daws. He had his network in place, vast and loyal. He would call on them and they would answer.

"Do you think this Daws is powerful enough to turn back Death?" Lady Yrris whispered. Everyone else's attention, including mine, was trained on Daws's back, trying to overhear some smidgen of his plan. Yrris spoke softly, not wanting anyone else to be a part of the conversation.

"I don't know, but our path here is fixed."

"Are you talking about destiny or fate? Forgive me, Phillip, but I don't believe in such things. I believe our choices have power."

"Oh, so do I. Choices might be the only thing in the universe with real power. Natural forces tend to follow mathematical laws, and those pesky things love a good average. So even in their most extreme, natural phenomena tend to balance themselves and eventually change very little.

"People making choices, however, reshape entire planets, carve empires out of the stars, and can bring all of it crashing back to rubble again. It's glorious and vibrant, watching humanity writhe against the averages." I paused a moment in my musings. "No, no. I would never suggest that you aren't in control of your own path. I'm only saying that I have reason to believe that the ending to this particular story is already set."

"And what is this reason? And what is this ending you speak of? Will my people be saved?" She asked the question in the same low, conversational tone, but her eyes betrayed her hunger for the answer.

While she was a powerful leader among her people, she still needed the same assurance they did. She desperately wanted someone to tell her that everything was going to be all right. Even if that person was someone with questionable sanity.

"I can't tell you the ending because I don't know it," I confessed. "But part of my nature is that I can't interfere with the story. Trying to affect a story causes me incredible… discomfort."

"But you have done so much already!" she protested. "You translate for us, you have traveled back through the Vortex, spoken to my people. And now you have given information to Daws that seems very important indeed…"

"Exactly," I interrupted her. I waited for the implications to sink in, but she continued to stare at me blankly. I finally offered her another piece to the puzzle. "Yes, I have done significant, story-changing things, and yet I feel no soul-rending chaos in my mind. So either I have suddenly gained new power, or…"

I leaned in and raised my eyebrows. This time the lights came on in her eyes, followed immediately by deep concern.

"Or they were not significant at all," she finished for me. I patted her on the back like a favored pupil and she continued. "That's why you believe the story ending is set. If you haven't changed the story by your actions, that means that Daws was always going to win, or was always going to lose, with or without you."

I nodded and continued staring at her. There was one more piece for her to put into place. To her credit, she got it quickly, though her shoulders drooped at the thought.

"And with or without me," she concluded. "The information I provided didn't change the story either. I thought this story was about my people, our chance for a better life, free from the Tanniks. Is it possible that we're just a part of Colonel Daws's story?"

"I admire your optimism, milady," I said, sincerely. She looked confused for a moment, then turned a shade paler.

"You mean that we're going to lose, don't you? You mean that what we have said and done doesn't matter because none of it was ever going to be enough to defeat the Tanniks."

I shook my head. "People are always trying to figure out what I mean. Somehow it always surprises them to discover that I mean exactly what I say. I have no agenda of my own on this world. I said I don't know and I truly don't.

"Yes, it's possible that there is nothing this technological world can do against the magic of the Tanniks. Or, there might be nothing the Tanniks can do against this world's technology. I'm only saying that when all is said and done, it's not even going to be close."

"Then I hope Daws is even more dangerous than you think," she whispered with deep conviction, no longer looking at me, but once again staring at the uniformed back across the room. "Defeating the Tanniks would make him the greatest hero our world has ever known. We would follow such a man forever."

"I do believe he's counting on that," I mumbled under my breath.

My comment wasn't quiet enough and she huffed at me. However, as she opened her mouth to scold me for my cynicism, we were interrupted by a crowd of people pushing their way into the room. Some were obviously flunkies of Colonel Daws, gathering their orders and rushing away again to carry out those orders.

Most, however, were workmen, wheeling in carts of materials and tools. The first wave started in with sledgehammers, slamming away at the wall farthest from the Vortex with reckless abandon.

Men with nicer shirts wrestled with large paper rolls of

building plans. They pointed here and there and murmured amongst each other, arguing over things like bearing walls, stress points, and tensile versus shear strength.

These engineers must have been little more than rubber stamps, however, as the workers didn't wait for their instruction nor permission as they dug into the job at hand. Already, half of the wall separating the two apartments was gone, the rubble loaded efficiently onto carts that disappeared as soon as they were loaded and were instantly replaced by empty ones.

As soon as the last of the rubble was cleared from where they first began, velvety cushioned chairs appeared as if by magic on top of an intricately woven area rug that covered the raw concrete scar that marked the previous location of the wall.

"Let's have you move over there," Lori told us, motioning to the open spot where a wall used to be, freshly cleared by the dedicated teams. "It's for your own protection."

Kip and Yrris moved over to the chairs quickly and willingly. Chuck mirrored Kip's own enthusiasm, though he didn't take a chair for himself. Rather, he stayed right by Kip's feet, like a loyal dog, or one who was afraid that he might have guns pointed at him again.

I remained long enough to make eye contact with Lori. I tilted my head ever so slightly as I raised an eyebrow. Nothing was said, but I knew she understood that I didn't buy this at face value. She, however, seemed rather unperturbed by my ominous stare and gestured for me again to take a seat.

The first crew wasn't even done taking apart the wall when the second crew started on its task: building a new one.

The new wall was being set between us and the Vortex. This wall was a vast improvement on the last wall. It was being put together with large, clear blocks. Each brick was a section of glass, so thick and reinforced that it would have taken a mortar shell to crack one.

Each brick was laid down by two grunting men. Then a third man layered a kind of mortar on all exposed edges of the brick. The mortar had a thick, sticky texture. I had little doubt that when cured, it would allow for slight movements, like rubber. That way, even incredible concussive forces could hit the wall and it would be able to shift and bend slightly without breaking.

Brick after brick was set into place by experienced hands. The wall rose like an opposing force to the Vortex across the room, solid where the Vortex was ethereal, man-made and technological where the Vortex was a creation of magic.

Lori took a less defensive pose as the wall took shape. She didn't have to stand guard anymore; we were sealed off from the Vortex, neatly, quietly, and all for our own protection. Lady Yrris sensed the impending isolation and some worry crept into her eyes, though when she saw me watching her, she glared her defiance at my suspicions.

"Why are you so against Colonel Daws?" she asked me in a whispered challenge. "If this place is about to be a battlefield, shouldn't we be protected? Would you have done anything differently?"

"This place isn't about to be a battlefield," I shook my head at her, though I offered no explanation. Everything would be clear soon enough. "Wait for the third crew."

"What…?" Yrris started, but was soon interrupted by the arrival of the third crew. They came in just as the last of the first crew were finishing up. The remnants of the old wall were cleared away and brooms were out, shuffling the final bits of dust and gravel out into the hallway.

Crunching over that last bit of rubble came men and women carrying padded cases. They pulled out tripods and expensive-looking machines. Cords, cables, and hoses ran from device to device. The web of connections terminated in the wall, fusing the network of instruments to the communications polymer network.

"What are those?" Yrris asked.

"That would be recording equipment," I hazarded a guess. "See the lenses there? And the things covered in the foam there I'm guessing are microphones of some sort. Give them another hundred years and they'll get all this equipment into something you can hold in one hand, but for now, you're looking at the most advanced video and audio recording equipment this world has to offer."

My explanation did nothing to ease the look of confusion on her face.

"Shouldn't there be weapons here instead? I understand a little of what you said, that these things will somehow keep a record of what happens here, but what are they here to record, exactly?"

"They are here to record your great hero, Colonel Daws, of course," I jabbed. "You didn't think he'd let an opportunity like this pass by, did you? The best kind of history is the kind with good sound and editing. It's a shame they haven't got color figured out yet."

"Now you're not making any sense at all, Phillip," Yrris scolded me, her voice rising above a whisper. "You don't seem crazy, but then you babble on about history and colors and changing sounds. How is anyone supposed to take you seriously?"

"Most don't," I admitted, "and that's probably just as well. History is often confusing until it is lived."

Lady Yrris rolled her eyes at me and snorted in a most unladylike fashion, turning away to talk to Kip. That turned out to be a very short-lived conversation, however, as she remembered that she needed me to translate and didn't feel like including me at the moment.

I took a moment to put my hand on the glass wall separating us from the Vortex. It wasn't cold. So it probably wasn't real glass, then. Likely some polymer they had developed. I wondered how strong it was. I would probably get a chance to discover that for myself very soon.

Chapter 8

People never jump from their morals. Corruption happens at a crawl, one compromise at a time.

–Musings of the Historian

The first few spots of darkness came through the portal like bits of ash, lazy and floating. They seemed no more dangerous than a bit of fluff.

Once the first few specks had wandered around the room a minute or two, the swarm came as a flood.

The room behind the glass went black in the time it took to draw a surprised gasp. Thousands of the tiny swarmlings tapped against the glass every second, creating a sharp crackle that continued like hail on a tin roof.

I leaned in to get a closer look at one of the tiny pieces of the swarm. I had expected something insect-like, like a wasp or bee, but these things bore no resemblance to that elegant design. They were black and bulbous, with no clear distinction as to which end was the front, back, top, or bottom. They looked more than anything like melted black glass, lumpy and scattered.

Still, they clearly lacked the hardness of glass and some of the things that hit too hard against the wall broke and oozed out an oily paste as they slid to the floor. It was a grotesque sight, but that thought only had an instant to flick across my mind before it was shoved to the side by a crushing realization of the size of this swarm.

The thousands, if not millions of swarmlings that pounded themselves into oblivion against our glass protector were absolutely nothing compared to the vast mass that pulsed through the room on the other side.

It gave the impression of a deep river, flowing fast out of the room, exploring the hallways and other rooms of the slum building. More rattling came from the door to the room in which we sat, but it had been thoroughly reinforced. Nothing could get in here.

That didn't stop the swarm from gushing through the building like a flood, exploring it, gutting it in an instant, and then pouring out of the building to the screams of passers-by.

We all rushed to the window then. The blackness gushed out onto street level and swept over the line of vehicles and soldiers that formed a loose barrier around the building. They were completely unprepared for an attack of this kind. They had been set there to keep people out. Many of the soldiers were still facing the wrong way when Death crashed into them.

Even in our fortified bunker three stories off the ground, we could hear the screams. The Tannik called Death was well-versed in his craft of spreading fear. One scream after another was cut short right at its loudest. The psychological effect on people nearby was devastating. Those who were far enough away so as to not get caught in the initial wave stampeded away in mindless panic. They shoved and trampled each other like cattle in their mad dash to get away from the horrifying sounds behind them.

It was a nightmare.

The swarmlings had left the room now, leaving behind only a few drifting spots of blackness. They were tiny sentries, left to keep an eye on us as the main swarm moved out to rampage and dominate.

Even Daws stood slack-jawed at the devastation, though not for long. The communicator on the wall chirped and demanded his attention. He waved a hand at Lori, who switched the communicator on, then hit another switch to channel it through a larger speaker, part of the recording equipment that had been brought in.

The call was a stream of reports, one right after another, all with a similar message. A dark swarm was pushing from building to building, ripping people apart. Shots were being fired into the mass by a few scattered policemen, but to no effect. A few of the swarmlings were struck and fell out of the main mass, but they were a few grains of sand. Worst of all, the swarm seemed to be growing with each new crowd it consumed.

"What are they saying?" Yrris asked me, tugging on my sleeve as her voice broke slightly.

"I suspect you know, Lady," I responded gravely. "They're saying that people are dying. The details are changing only by location. Death is providing the kind of shock and awe the Tanniks will need to cow this people into submission."

"So we've lost, then?" Those four words carried a world in them. Her heart was breaking in that moment. "It looks like you were right after all. It was never going to be a close contest."

I shook my head.

"Look at Daws," I offered. She looked around and found him standing at the window, looking out at the city while the reports played behind him. It was the very image of a thoughtful man.

"Does that look like a man who has given up? Does it even look like a very shocked man?"

"No," she admitted.

"This is a battle for domination of two worlds. Did you think it would be bloodless? This is only the first move. I wouldn't bet against Daws just yet."

"Then what is he waiting for?" she demanded. "It's not very heroic of him to stand there, watching people die!"

"This is a different kind of hero, Lady, one who's not going to let emotions push him into any rash decisions. He's playing the long game."

"So what's his next move? What is he waiting for?"

"He's waiting for someone to ask him nicely."

"What?!" Yrris exclaimed. "You must be joking! Our plight couldn't be more serious. Does he want me to beg?"

Her eyes filled with tears.

"Because I'll do it. If he needs someone to beg, then I'll get down on my knees. If he needs loyalty, I'll pledge myself and my people to him for all time. I'll do whatever I have to in order to save my people. What you see out there is only the beginning. We've crossed the Tanniks.

"Death is having his fun for now, but he'll be coming after my people next. We will be punished for trying to leave, and with this new world of slaves at their disposal, they won't be worried about conserving the population, they'll let Death have full sway."

"I believe you," I soothed her. "And I suspect you will have a key role to play in all this, but not now. Someone does need to beg, you're right about that. You can hold on to your dignity for now, however. Daws has other goals in mind and I think we'll get to see them soon."

As if I'd summoned the event by predicting it, the reports coming in from the speaker ceased suddenly. Daws turned from the window to look at Lori, who had been screening the calls, transferring from one call to another like a seasoned reporter.

She nodded. The call they had been waiting on had come in.

He moved to sit down at a chair in the center of the room. Technicians quietly adjusted cameras and microphones. The stage was set and the show was about to begin, all of it captured for posterity.

Lori flipped a switch and a low buzz announced the open communication line.

"Greetings, Sir Minister. How may I be of service?" Daws's voice fairly oozed with eager obedience. The voice on the other side blustered and huffed, a diplomat caught in a situation running out of control.

"Colonel Daws, where are you? I'm hearing reports I can't believe. Are we under attack? Has the Alliance developed some new weapon? What are you doing about this?"

The questions came one on top of another, not waiting for an answer. Daws expertly waited for the Minister to pause for breath, then jumped in with his explanations.

"It is an attack, Sir Minister, but not from the Alliance. A portal has opened from another world and a being of immense power has come through. That is what is sweeping over our troops and killing our citizens."

A dull hum of electricity played an ominous background to the silence that answered Daws's report. I could imagine the man on the other end, swarthy and soft from years of office work and chamber meetings with other important people. His jaw would be opening and closing, but with no words as his mind raced. He would process this outlandish information, weighing it against everything he knew about Daws.

In many ways, it was a kind of contest. On one side, there

was the undeniable fact that such a thing could not exist. Portals from other worlds? Alien beings wreaking havoc in the city? Such things were impossible. The logical mind knew that and would reject anything that said otherwise. That's why the most educated minds are often the most closed to revolutionary ideas.

On the other side of the scales would be Daws's reputation. In this case, it had to be substantial indeed. In the months I'd lived here, I'd heard of the Minister. He was the head of the Oligarchy, a council of seven men and women who held all the real power in the government. There was an elected senate that could pass laws, but the Oligarchy had such intricate veto powers that it could change any law to suit its own ends. The Oligarchy ruled the Senate, and the Minister ruled the Oligarchy.

And now the Minister, in the nation's moment of crisis, was calling a colonel.

That fact spoke volumes of how much Daws had done to build his foundation. Now the Minister would come to the only conclusion he could. Daws was telling the truth and his nation was at war. His next sentence showed exactly that.

"What can we do?" All the bluster was gone, the authority erased in the humility of fear and uncertainty.

"I'm confident that General Hines is doing everything that can be done, Sir Minister. I have secured the building where the portal is and I am awaiting his orders."

There was a sound like a mix of a scoff and a disgusted spit on the other end of the line.

"Don't be naïve, Colonel," the Minister scolded. "You are far too bright to trust a moment like this to someone like Hines. He's related to four of the seven Oligarchs and he's a fine man, but he has little combat experience. He was a gifted administrator during the war, but we would never have made him High General if it weren't peacetime. You have to take command."

"Sir Minister," responded Daws meekly, "as much as I respect you, I cannot do that. Military code dictates that a colonel cannot take control of the army unless all generals have been incapacitated. General Hines is alive and healthy, as well as three other generals in this city alone who serve under him. It would take an act of the Senate to promote me to High General, and I have far too much respect for General Hines to displace him in such a rough manner."

A frustrated growl rumbled over the speaker.

"Your military etiquette be hanged, Colonel! We don't have time for Senate hearings, we need you now! I am commanding you to take control of the armies."

"What's going on?" Yrris tugged at my sleeve and whispered. "It doesn't sound much like begging to me! Sounds more like anger."

"That's because you've never heard a government beg. The Minister is trying to make Colonel Daws a general in charge of the armies. Our Colonel is refusing."

"Why would he refuse? Haven't you been saying he is going to take power? Why wouldn't he accept it when offered?"

"It's quite simple. They haven't reached his price yet. Now let me listen, I promise I'll fill in all the details for you after the conversation."

She nodded her acceptance of the deal and I turned my attention back to the negotiation unfolding in the center of the room.

"...because it's illegal, Sir Minister. With all due respect, I cannot be a part of something that would undermine the very core of our society. Our laws must be followed, even when we're afraid, or they are not laws at all."

The Minister groaned. I could almost hear him pulling at whatever hair he had left. Then, as was bound to happen, the good Minister got a brilliant idea.

Chapter 9

The ultimate form of persuasion is getting the other person to come up with your idea.

–Musings of the Historian

"What if you weren't a General at all?" The Minister's voice was suddenly brighter and he spoke more quickly, as if the idea would vanish if he didn't give it shape fast enough.

"We could make you the Commissioner! You'd have to leave the military, of course, as the Commissioner is a civilian position, but it would put even the High General under your authority, and under wartime powers, you could command troops directly."

"Commissioner?" Daws said the word like it was the first time he had heard it. "The head of the Intelligence Commission? Wasn't that position dissolved after the war? It was only ever supposed to be a temporary measure."

"That's just the thing!" The Minister's voice was flushed with victory now. He'd struggled a bit with the earlier conversation, but now he'd seen a way to get the right person in charge without offending his high ideals. "We did release the last Commissioner, Kelson York, as soon as the war was done, but the position itself was never dissolved. Between you and me, most of us didn't trust York with that much power. But you'd be perfect! I've always said your talents were wasted, supervising researchers and pencil pushers in those labs."

"I'll confess it would solve our current predicament," Daws admitted grudgingly. "Still, my understanding is that an appointment of that level would take a unanimous vote by the Oligarchy. I suspect Oligarch Nelson would object to my appointment."

"Nelson can be made to see reason," the Minister intoned ominously. He was feeling back in power again and wasn't afraid to wield that power now that he saw a clear path to salvation. "Besides, she wouldn't dare stand up to the remaining six if we're all united. And who better to be Commissioner than the Hero of Falkirk?"

"You honor me, Minister. I doubt there are many who remember that anymore," Daws demurred.

"Bah! Why do you think we're talking right now? I need that ingenuity, that natural command. Your country needs it, son. Will you do this for us? For me?"

Daws paused. It was a beautiful pause, a masterful pause. I had no doubt that history students in the future would write essays about that pause. It was a pause that gave proper reverence to the request and all it implied.

"If the Oligarchy truly does vote unanimously, then I will serve at their will and direction, Minister."

There was the distinct sound of a slap on the other end, the Minister slapping his own knee in triumph.

"Magnificent! I will get back to you shortly. Please, I know you don't want to show any disrespect to General Hines, but I beg you to start taking steps. I will have your appointment finalized as fast as I can. History will forgive you for getting an early start."

"I will await your confirmation," Daws said firmly. The Minister sighed, then signed off. Daws sat rigid in his chair for a silent three seconds before waving to his men to shut off the cameras.

"Congratulations, Colonel," Lori beamed brightly at Colonel Daws. The moment was enough for even Daws to smile and nod back at her. That was the entire celebration.

Yrris was tugging on my sleeve again.

"The meeting is over, tell me what happened now."

"The government handed the army and the country over to our Colonel."

"Really? Wow. Were they angry that he demanded such a high price for his service?"

I chuckled.

"You keep underestimating Daws. No, they weren't angry, they were grateful."

"Grateful?"

"Oh yes, they begged him to take control and he let them persuade him. Now the real battle begins. They'll hand the reins over, but if he doesn't deliver, they'll rip him to shreds."

"What does it all mean, Phillip?" Yrris asked, her emotions were ragged and raw.

"It means you have your dangerous man."

***

The confirmation was as sure as the Minister had predicted. Whatever Oligarch Nelson had against Daws wasn't enough to stop the Oligarchy from handing over all the special powers of a wartime autocrat.

"You now have full command of our troops and resources, Commissioner Daws. All of our best wishes go with you. For reasons of safety, the other Oligarchs and I are moving to Shelter B. You can communicate with us there."

And with no more fanfare than that, Colonel Daws became Commissioner Daws, leader of a nation in all but name.

"Time to get to work. Lori, get me Tratch."

Tratch turned out to be the name of the young aide who Daws had sent away shortly after learning of the time difference. What he had been doing all this time, I couldn't imagine. Lori turned to the communicator, but was interrupted by Tratch himself entering the room carrying several glass boxes.

Each box had a cover over it so we couldn't see what was inside.

"Commissioner Daws, sir!" Tratch saluted sharply, somehow already knowing about Daws's promotion. "I have samples and I'm ready to begin testing."

"Excellent work, Tratch. Let's get this started."

Tratch whipped the covers off of the boxes. Each one contained several of the swarmlings we had seen earlier.

"What have we seen as far as its intelligence out in the field, Tratch?"

"It is incredibly adaptive, sir. It recognizes threats and attacks viciously. Still, its actions show a kind of laziness."

"Laziness?"

"Yes, sir. It is not used to any sort of resistance at all. It attacks head on and uses brute force to overwhelm our forces. Further, while we know that it can maintain contact with these individual units over some distance, it is not choosing to do so. The whole swarm has continued to stay together, with few exceptions."

"Glad to hear it, Tratch. Has it tried to communicate at all?"

"We suspect so. There have been specific noise patterns that have repeated. I suspect it is giving a warning of some kind, but we lack a translator of our own. Perhaps if Phillip..."

His eyes drifted to me as he started his suggestion, but Daws cut him off.

"No. I can't spare him just yet. I took a big enough risk altering the apartment. I dare not take him further from here. Try and get some recordings, if you can."

"Very well, sir. I will commence my testing now."

Each glass box had a complicated system of hatches and gears on top of it. Tratch moved quickly and effectively, placing various items in small spaces on top of each lid, then turning a crank that shifted the mechanisms within the device.

The effect was that he was able to put things into the box without ever opening it or creating a path to the outside for the swarmlings within.

Each tiny package seemed to act like a tiny bomb as soon as it got into the glass box. One erupted in flame, the next spewed foul green fumes, and the next emitted a pink gas so light that I had to lean forward to tell that anything had happened at all.

The most interesting one, to my mind, was a small device that dropped in, and at first, seemed to do nothing at all. Then, I noticed a very low sound that increased in frequency, rising in pitch until finally going beyond what we could hear.

At two different points, the small swarmlings inside the box reacted strongly to the noises, rattling wildly at their enclosure before quieting down again as the frequency box moved on.

At the end of the experiment, most of the swarmlings lay lifeless at the bottom of their boxes. Some even smoked or bubbled.

"Looks like we have some options," Daws commented. Tratch nodded eagerly.

"These things might look all kinds of scary in a swarm, but they are susceptible to heat, acid, and blunt force. They showed some distress at certain vibrations, but nothing fatal, it would appear."

"Very well," Daws nodded curtly, "I trust your forces are prepared."

"Yes, sir!" Nothing could disguise the enthusiasm in Tratch's voice.

"Then let's get this thing summoned back in here."

Tratch snapped his fingers at two soldiers standing by the door. They moved quickly to rigid boxes that had been placed with the rest of the equipment and supplies. In less than a minute, both men had suited up in a kind of biochemical armor. Each fitting was airtight, and the helmet was a massive affair that had an array of filters and small machines attached on all sides.

Whatever they were going to do took no further orders than the snap of Tratch's fingers and the two of them left the room and reappeared back in the other half of the room, where Kip and I had lived. The swarmlings that had remained behind had been flitting about randomly in a kind of holding pattern.

Now they focused in on the two men, hovering around them like flies. The pair took several trips back and forth from the hallway, bringing in box after box of the curious glass bricks that formed the wall that even now divided us from the Vortex.

They started placing the glass blocks in a pattern arcing out from the two walls. When the two arcs met, the intent became clear.

They were walling off the Vortex.

The small swarmlings started to buzz and dip around the men. Several of them smacked into the two men, but whatever attack the swarmlings used to rip regular men to shreds had no effect on the jointed armor worn by the two workers.

"Let's get those reports going again, Lori," Daws spoke in a low voice, his attention riveted on the two workers in the other room. With a few clicks and switches, more voices streamed into the room. The swarm was leaving, they said. It was headed back to the first building, the building Daws was in even now.

We all rushed back to the window to look out. Sure enough, a dark mass coalesced out of the surrounding buildings like the thick smoke that comes out of a volcano before eruption. Once gathered, it seemed to stretch and pulse as it raced toward our location.

"Two minutes," Tratch said. More men rushed from the room. Already we could feel, more than hear, the low roar of the approaching swarm. As mind-numbingly large as the swarm had appeared before, it was even larger now. It dwarfed the buildings around it as it washed over them, approaching our location.

"So… it's coming here, right?" asked Chuck.

"Yup, it would appear that way," Kip answered.

"And it kills people?"

"Yes. I'd say a great many people have died today."

"Any word on how it treated plants?"

Kip chuckled and placed a hand tenderly on a leaf. "I'm sure it has no interest in plants and will leave you alone."

It was a touching moment, seeing that man comforting his plant. A psychiatrist would have been quick to point out that it was merely a cyclical transference. Kip was talking to the plant, but since the plant was part of his delusion, he was really talking to himself, trying to reassure himself in the face of imminent danger, like any other person would.

To avoid such observations, I try to spend as little time as possible around psychiatrists.

The building shook as the newly enlarged swarm roared its way in. It was like a giant, returning to its cave in the morning, having gorged itself all night on the local flocks.

The two men in the other room, having finished their hasty wall, hurried back into our makeshift bunker and slammed the door closed behind them, just as the swarm arrived. Every cubic centimeter of space was packed with swarmlings as the main bulk crammed itself into the Vortex room.

Kip lifted Chuck into his arms and backed slowly away from the glass wall. Even Daws took a small step back as the wall creaked ever so slightly.

Lady Yrris, however, had quite the opposite reaction. She stepped forward and spoke to the swarm.

"See me, Death!" she cried. "Do I tremble before you? See me! Do I obey your rumblings? See me and despair, you scattering of dust. Your power is broken today."

"What is she saying?" Daws gripped my arm and pulled me back to yell in my ear over the roaring noise of the swarm.

"She's challenging his power. She's saying she's not afraid of him."

"Impressive," he whispered. "And useful…"

He turned to Tratch, who was huddled up with the communicator, still receiving reports from the outside.

"Is the swarm entirely inside the building?" he asked. When Tratch nodded his head, Daws commanded, "Seal the openings."

Far in the distance, there were clangs and crashes as barriers were thrown against every opening. Tratch and Daws's men had not been idle in their given time. As Daws had hoped,

Death did not notice, being distracted by the spectacle of the defiant Lady Yrris.

A thrumming sound pulsed against the glass, growing louder. For a moment, I thought it was some kind of sonic attack, then something clicked in my mind and I recognized what it was...

Laughter.

Chapter 10

Heroic deeds have a lot to do with recognizing the right moment.
-Musings of the Historian

The huge swarm acted like an enormous speaker. Even protected by the thick glass wall and layers of concrete, the sound pulsed in our very bones. The voice that followed was just as penetrating.

"I HAVE RULED YOU PITIFUL SLAVES FOR CENTURIES." Everywhere around me, people clapped hands to their heads, trying to block out some small portion of the sound that shook them to the core. "COUNTLESS HUMANS HAVE STOOD BEFORE ME UNAFRAID, THINKING IT COURAGE. IT IS ONLY A SIGN OF THEIR IGNORANCE."

A hand on my arm demanded my attention.

"Is it speaking?" Daws yelled into my ear. I nodded affirmatively.

"It's about what you'd expect. Turns out it's awesome and powerful and we're weak and insignificant."

"You're right. That's exactly what I was expecting. Should I say something back?"

"This is your show, Daws. Give your lines as you like. It won't understand you, though, and emotional, defiant speeches tend to lose a lot of their oomph when they have to pause for translation."

"You know, Phillip, about half the time, you half make

72

sense. I guess I'll leave it to Lady Yrris, she seems like she's got this well in hand. The microphones couldn't pick up anything with this much noise anyway."

Lady Yrris did, in fact, have the defiance part well under control. Tears streamed down her face, but it was only the emotional catharsis of her fury.

"You arrogant filth!" she screamed at the gathered blackness. "Your centuries have only made you fat and weak. You bully those who have already been ground into nothing. Well, no more! NO MORE!"

Her throat was being savaged by the sheer volume of her yelling, but as her voice caught and grew hoarse, she only bore down harder.

"You see around you what humanity is capable of, independent of your smothering. My people will know this freedom even if I have to crush you myself, bug by bug! But I will be denied that pleasure, you twisted monster. Your doom happens here and now. I will watch and laugh as you fall at the hands of humanity's champion, Colonel Daws!"

She turned and pointed at Daws in triumphant exultation. Daws immediately looked to me for the meaning behind the gesture.

"She says her new boyfriend can beat it up," I offered.

"Phillip, you're a lousy translator," Daws deadpanned.

"That's probably true. Still, if you've had enough time to enact your plan and were looking for a cue, that was it."

"Fair enough," Daws answered. "On my signal, Tratch. Roll the cameras, we'll get what we can."

Daws stepped forward, right up to the glass. More of the pulsing rhythm of laughter shook the glass, but this time Daws gave no ground. He raised his right hand, palm open and forward, as if he could push the swarm back by his will alone. For all the coldness of his calculations, his voice was strong and passionate as he roared back at Death.

"You have invaded our world. You think us weak because you caught us by surprise. Witness the truth now in your final moments. We are not slaves… We are not afraid… And we are not weak!"

At the last syllable, he clenched his hand into a fist, twisting it in the air like he was wielding a sword. Out of the corner of my eye, I saw Tratch talking into a microphone. Timed right along with the symbol of the clenched fist came a new roar. Red and orange flame erupted into the Vortex room. Creaking from outside our own sealed door revealed the immense pressures at work.

While Yrris was yelling her defiance at Death, Tratch and his men had been pumping the hallways full of a colorless, odorless, and flammable gas. At the signal from Daws, they had ignited it. The effect was equal to any level of elemental majesty the Tanniks could have brought to bear. Fire filled the building, sucking oxygen from the air and heating everything to infernal destruction.

One form of blackness shifted to another as the massive swarm in front of us was engulfed in flame, then the glass wall itself was covered in ash and char and everything was hidden from our view.

Daws turned and ran back to where Tratch hovered over the communicator. It was the first time I had seen true urgency in the man. He normally exuded a sense of control and calm, but in that moment of his trap springing, he was unsure.

74

Yrris staggered back into a chair, her emotions spent with her tirade and the dramatic eruption of flame engulfing the ancient enemy of her people. She waved me over while Daws chattered with Tratch behind us.

"What did Daws say, there at the end?"

"He apologized very sweetly, but said that today wasn't a good time for an invasion."

"Phillip, you're a lousy translator."

"Yeah, I keep hearing that, but I still feel pretty good about my job security. Not a lot of other people lining up for the job."

"What is 'job security'?" she asked, puzzled.

"Ah yes, I suppose job security is not a concept slaves run into much. Job security is when you're not afraid of someone else taking your work away from you."

"Now you're being silly on purpose. Why would anyone…"

A thump rattled against the glass wall. As one, every head in the room snapped to look at the spot. Another thump, this one louder and focused, produced visible motion in one of the bricks.

"The sad sucker survived," Tratch cursed. He turned and started talking into the communicator, getting another charge of gas ready. Back at the wall, however, the thumping was growing louder.

This wasn't the general pressure of a swarm. This was the insistent, focused attack of an enemy intent on getting through. With each thump, it was clear that the entire force was being focused on one single brick, and the effort was paying off. Already, the brick was visibly dislodged.

"What's happening?" Kip and Yrris spoke at the same time. I smiled maniacally at both of them.

"Death made his move, threw his weight around. Then

Daws made his move and threw his weight around. Now blood has been spilt on both sides. The time for posturing is over."

"So what happens now?" screamed Chuck.

"Now, my dear plant," I leaned in and spoke barely above a whisper to the potted broadleaf, just loud enough for Yrris and Kip to overhear. "Now, a fight breaks out."

Men and women scrambled, grabbing key equipment and heading for the window. Expert hands plied tools at the hinges and the window fell free, crashing loudly three stories below. Ropes were going over the side when the first glass brick fell free.

Tratch and Daws were both ready with their weapons and the second the brick fell through. Daws fired. I understood then that he had actually undersold the destructive power of his weapon. To fire it, he had to brace himself to absorb the recoil.

It was like someone holding onto a rocket. The steady stream of chemically strengthened flame contacted the swarm trying to get through from the other side.

Swarmlings charred and fell like volcanic ash from the opening. As long as Daws and Tratch could keep up that stream, Death would not be getting through.

Still, the loss of a brick was catastrophic. The other bricks above the fallen one now sagged ever so slightly, a sign of weakness that Death was quick to exploit. New thumping started on the other bricks, this time acting even faster on the weakened wall.

"Changing in three… two… one!" yelled Daws. Tratch started firing his weapon as Daws said "two" and kept the flame flowing steadily into the breach. Daws dropped to one knee, propping the gun on his leg as he ejected the spent gas cartridge and slipped in a new one. A latch drove the new cartridge into place and locked it. He stood up next to Tratch, ready to take his next turn as soon as Tratch's flamethrower ran low on fuel. The weapons were impressive, but the gas ran out quickly.

"We are on to Plan B, people, let's get this room cleared!" Daws roared, sweat now streaming down his face. "Tratch, we're going to need a dummy gun in this spot in forty seconds. Switching back in three… two…"

Daws started firing with his freshly-loaded flame gun and Tratch turned quickly to the boxes behind them that had been left by the crew. He shoved three of the heaviest of them over near the wall, as close as he could get without being in Daws's line of fire.

The two larger boxes he pushed together on his gun, pinching it between the two boxes so they held it pointing at the breach in the wall. The smaller box he positioned behind the gun, so that the recoil wouldn't spoil the aim. Tratch's quick hands applied rope and some kind of adhesive and the whole thing solidified into a makeshift gun-vise.

"Dummy gun is ready, sir!" Tratch yelled.

"Good!" Daws responded. "Wait until everyone is out. On my mark."

Nearly everyone was already out at that point. Soldiers had rappelled down the side of the building first to secure the ends of the ropes and set up a belay. Now Kip, Yrris, and I were being fitted with harnesses that clipped onto the ropes.

One of the soldiers tried to get Kip to let go of Chuck, but the ensuing struggle wasted enough time that Daws turned and yelled at the soldier.

"Let him take the bloody plant!"

Once he knew that Chuck wasn't going to be taken away from him, Kip was much more amenable to letting the soldier get his harness on.

Once the harnesses were in place, they clipped onto the ropes leading out of the window and we were unceremoniously shoved out, the rate of our descent controlled by the soldiers below.

Kip yelped and clung to Chuck even tighter, which only served to make the ride down harder on both of them, as Kip didn't pay attention to pushing off the building with his legs and instead rode all the way down bumping off the building like a ball on a string. The rough ride shook a lot of dirt out of Chuck's pot and the two of them reached the ground looking awfully ragged.

We were instantly hurried away as soon as our feet touched the ground. There were armored vehicles surrounding the building to keep people away. The soldiers who had originally manned these were dead, swept away in Death's first attack, though no bodies remained to mark their final moments. Now Tratch's chosen men escorted us quickly to a spot behind one of these bulky contraptions.

Finally, out of the window came Tratch and Daws, rappelling down the side of the building barely slower than a freefall. They hit the ground running.

"Blow it!" shouted Daws, "Blow it now!"

Deafening booms echoed his shouted order, and the entire building shook behind them. As the two of them made the line of armored trucks, a second round of explosions erupted flames from all the lower windows and doors and the entire building began to fall under its own weight. The massive slum building crashed to the ground, thousands of tons of fiber-reinforced concrete shaking the ground under us with the impact.

"LAUNCH!" Daws screamed the order over the roar of the

falling building. From several locations around the building, projectiles launched in a burst of flame, arced gracefully over the wreckage, then exploded in mid-air, raining the wreckage in burning napalm.

"LAUNCH AGAIN!" Even as he roared the command, several of us watching the wreckage thought we could imagine some of the darker smoke starting to pull together, trying to regain some cohesion after the violence of the crash and fire. If swarm it was, it was a pitifully small swarm, barely bigger than a barrel, but all of us knew how quickly it could grow if even one swarmling survived.

Just as the tiny swarm started to gain a presence, the second round of projectiles burst overhead. This time, the rain wasn't napalm. Clear liquid, like water, came down in a mist. The sun refracted through the vapor and cast a perfect rainbow. It was a bizarrely beautiful scene, the vibrant colors hanging just above the hungry flames and heat distortions.

It was as if after starting the fire, they were trying to put it out with a light misting of water. However, it was painfully clear that this substance was not water. Where it touched, it hissed and burned. The tiny swarm that had risen out of the destruction of the fire was touched by the mist and fell almost immediately back onto the flames, tiny wisps of smoke being the only evidence that it had ever tried to share the same space as that caustic liquid.

"And launch," Daws said in a normal voice now, feeling his victory more assured. A third wave of projectiles arced, exploded, and the building was once again washed in sticky, burning napalm.

Billows of dark smoke rose straight into the air, a funeral pyre for a Tannik.

Chapter 11

It is a dark thing when the cold logic of science is applied to human populations. The pure numbers would suggest that some people are disposable.

–Musings of the Historian

"Tratch."

"Yes, sir!"

"Arm your men with the flame guns. Maintain active patrols, expanding and contracting circles. I want this wreckage extinguished and swept for any remaining pieces of the swarm. Be thorough."

"Yes, sir!"

It hadn't escaped me how much joy Tratch had taken in all the incredible destruction that had occurred. Each wave of devastation invigorated the man.

I now understood Tratch's role in Daws's entourage. Daws had not set up this sequence of destruction, Tratch had. I wondered idly how many more steps had been in place, if the building fire, demolition, and alternating waves of fire and acid hadn't worked.

"Lori."

"Yes, sir?"

"Analyze, please."

"Yes, sir. The primary swarm is undoubtedly destroyed. There might be small remnants somewhere, but I don't think we need to worry about them."

"Why do you say that?" Daws asked, surprised. "Seems like even one of these things could grow back into a huge swarm almost overnight."

"In theory, it could, sir, but I don't think it's that simple. We saw the swarm act as a unit and with intelligence. Also, it kept the mass fairly close together, even though it could have accomplished more by splitting into multiple swarms.

"This suggests that the intelligence was part of the swarm itself, each piece acting like a single neuron in a huge brain. We've destroyed enough of the swarm that I don't believe small units could still be capable of the complexity of interaction it would take to form intelligence.

"I feel this conclusion is supported by the evidence of the small swarm we saw rise out of the building. They had the instinct to gather together and away from danger, but then they hung in the air until the acid hit.

"We witnessed the large swarm act with decisive intelligence, even speech. The damaged swarm after the hallway detonation seemed more animal in its approach, hammering recklessly at the wall. Finally, the small swarm showed almost no intelligence at all."

"So you're saying we've killed the brain part of the swarm?" Daws clarified. Lori nodded in her reserved way.

"It would be more accurate to say that the swarm itself was the brain, sir. We've eliminated enough of the mass that the remaining pieces will not be capable of intelligent action. We should be able to track down and eliminate the remainder with little more trouble than it would take to exterminate a small infestation of insects."

"Excellent! Arrange a nationwide broadcast on the communication network. Tell the people that if they see any more of the creatures, to attack and kill them. If they see a swarm larger than their own head, have them contact the military and we'll come in with flame guns and armor suits."

"It will be done, sir," Lori nodded curtly. "And what would you like to do about the Vortex?"

"Hmm?" Daws mumbled, turning to look at the wreckage behind him. "Oh yes, I suppose we'd better see to that, hadn't we?"

Hanging thirty feet in the air, half concealed by the smoke, but still warping the air around it, was the Vortex.

"Phillip, do you still understand me?" Daws turned on me.

"Far better than you would like, Commissioner," I responded. He grunted at my wry response.

"And can you still understand Lady Yrris?"

Lady Yrris, hearing her name, perked up.

"What did he say?" she asked me.

"He wants to know if you're all right."

She beamed. Daws actually blushed a little as I asked the question he should have been asking.

"Tell him I'm fine, better than fine! He destroyed a Tannik! You were right about everything, Phillip, I can't believe…"

"She says thanks," I translated, succinctly.

"I don't appreciate being interrupted, Phillip," she fumed at me.

"Yes, I imagine so, but I felt like I'd gotten the broad strokes of what you were trying to say."

"And you came up with 'thanks'?!"

"Indeed!" I exulted over my own cleverness. "You were trying to express gratitude, I conveyed gratitude. Done and done."

82

"You know, Phillip," observed Daws. "I notice that your translations are usually much shorter than the original message."

"Right?!" I answered. "You're welcome!"

Both Yrris and Daws groaned at my upbeat assessment of my translating skills. Daws squared off to me, however.

"I need you to translate this directly, though. Ask Lady Yrris how long it would take her to move her people through the Vortex."

I stared at him dumbly for a moment. This was an unexpected move, and it's not often I am surprised by people. There had to be something I was missing.

Obediently, my mind racing, I turned and translated the question to Yrris word for word. Her eyes brimmed with grateful tears as she answered.

"With Death abroad, everyone will be gathered to the villages. We don't have much in the way of possessions, so we could probably get everyone through in a week if we start right away."

"She says everyone could get through in a week."

"Really?" mused Daws. "That's significantly less than I expected. Things must be worse than I thought if their population is that low."

I nodded my agreement. A population that size was more like a holding pattern, making sure humanity had enough genetic diversity in the gene pool to stay robust, but no more. It was a cold kind of logic that would use math and science to govern growth like a herd of cattle.

It sickened me.

"Lori," Daws was back in command mode. "Alert the engineers that I need access to that portal immediately. I need it enclosed again as well."

Lori scurried away to follow his orders as fast as she could.

I was amazed at the efficiency showed by their military engineers. Heavy, slow-moving motorized carts showed up in less than half an hour, groaning and grinding under the weight of building materials.

Lady Yrris, Kip, Chuck, and I gossiped like wide-eyed children about each new development. I translated for Lady Yrris and Kip translated for Chuck.

"Look at the size of those concrete blocks! It would take twenty of my most powerful stone movers to move even one of those," Yrris exclaimed.

"I'm guessing it will only take one man," I suggested.

"That's right," Kip added, pointing to one of the larger carts. "That's a deconstructed crane. I saw them used during the war. They used them to create shelters when we knew a big gas attack was coming. Those crane operators are artists.

"I never understood how they could put them together so quickly without anyone guiding them to make sure their lines were straight. We on the ground would help with the fastening and sealing and all that, of course."

"A bunch of human foolishness if you ask me," Chuck huffed. "You don't see us plants worrying about sealing stuff up or straight lines. The only plants that even get close to using straight lines are trees, and we all know they're a bunch of pretentious bullies and blowhards."

"Oh my, they're putting it together so fast," Yrris exulted. "We've always valued magical strength on our world, but I begin to wonder if it's been a crutch that kept us weak."

"And another thing about trees," Chuck ranted on,

84

interrupting my translation of what Yrris had said, "is how they take all the sunlight before it can get to us on the ground. And then they mock us for being small! That's why I like humans so much, in spite of your off behavior."

"Because we don't look down on you?" I asked.

"No! Because you cut down trees! That'll show the brutes, not so big now, are you…"

"That's enough, Chuck," I interrupted. "You're upsetting Kip."

Sure enough, as he "translated" Chuck's tirade, Kip got more and more red in the face. I also noticed that he kept glancing towards Daws and the other officers that were commanding the common soldiers in the massive building project.

Yrris patted Kip on the back and he settled down and smiled at her gratefully.

Meanwhile, a building of sorts was taking shape behind us. Fiber scaffolding clicked together like puzzle pieces and formed much of the inside, providing stairs, floors, and walls, depending on how they were put together. On the outside of this scaffolding, a newly assembled crane used immense counterbalances to lift heavy concrete slabs off the materials carts and place them upright.

Soldiers waited anxiously with tools and fasteners and as soon as the crane had a slab lowered into position, they leapt into action, securing the slab to the scaffolding using a myriad of hooks that had been built into the slab when it was poured.

By the time the team had the slab anchored securely, the crane was already bringing a new one over, and the process repeated. New crews came behind and applied mortar and sealant to any airspace left by the rough construction. Their swift and steady motion spoke of vast experience. These men and women were veterans, and they had learned these skills in a setting where their lives and the lives of all around them depended on it.

"Lady Yrris." We'd been so engrossed in watching the construction that we didn't notice Daws had returned from directing everything and now stood behind us. We all jumped a little in surprise. "The internal structure is secure up to the third floor now. We can access the Vortex. I recommend we go through and find your people. Phillip, translate."

"Yeah, yeah, yeah," I grumbled before translating his suggestion to Lady Yrris, who nodded enthusiastically. The nodding needed no translation, so I took the moment to chide Daws. "You know, eventually, you're going to have to learn her language. I can't coddle you people forever."

To my surprise, Daws nodded seriously at my chiding. "We've been recording as much as possible every time she speaks and when you translate. These recordings are being delivered to our very best linguists, who have been analyzing the language. We're hoping to have some basics down in a few days."

I stared back, flabbergasted. I had seen various underlings coming and going, looking busy, but I hadn't given them much thought.

"I need to stop underestimating you, Daws," I murmured. He smiled.

"Feel free to underestimate me all you want. Only understand that I won't be returning the favor, Phillip." He said my assumed name like an accusation. "Shall we be on our way?"

He motioned to Lady Yrris and she followed eagerly. I started to follow and he put a hand on my chest, stopping me.

"I don't think Lady Yrris will need a translator to manage her own people. I think it would be better if you stayed here."

Like ghosts appearing out of a mist, two soldiers with drawn weapons appeared at both sides of me. It looked like I wouldn't be joining this trip. Out of the corner of my eye, I could also see soldiers quietly discouraging Kip from picking up Chuck and following as well.

We sat and watched as Daws and Yrris walked toward the forming building. As they walked, other men filled in around them. These were not obvious soldiers. They had a variety of hairstyles and clothing. A careful look showed bulges of weapons stashed around their bodies, but out of plain sight. Their smooth, balanced way of walking looked like a tiger stalking prey and betrayed long years of combative training.

Men of this kind could be found on any world with large armies. They were the special forces, trained elite. They wouldn't have the standard military polish. Rather, they would strive to look as normal as possible. Regular soldiers marching in long rows and stiff uniforms were a show of force. These men Daws had around him now were no show, but real and effective force, disguised as a group of casual friends going for a walk.

The outer walls of the building were not yet complete, so we could see through as Daws and Yrris climbed the scaffolding within. They finally made their way to the portal and stepped through, disappearing from our view.

Chapter 12

Love creates absolutes.

> –Musings of the Historian

"Did you need anything?"

Kip and I jumped again. This time, it was Lori who had snuck up on us as our attention had been focused on the procession.

"Huh?" Kip responded in his normal eloquent fashion.

"Commissioner Daws instructed me to make sure you were comfortable. If there is anything you need, let me know and I'll be happy to arrange it.

"I'd like to go for a walk," I smiled cheerfully, flicking my eyes meaningfully towards the Vortex, now barely visible through the web of scaffolding and the rising wall of concrete.

"I'm afraid that's quite impossible," Lori bobbed her head in apology. "Commissioner Daws was most insistent that both of you remain in the area."

"Both of us?" Kip asked. "But there are three of us. What about Chuck?"

Lori didn't miss a beat as she responded completely straight-faced.

"We felt confident that Chuck's loyalty to you would ensure that he would also remain here if you did, Kip."

"Well in that case, I'd like some water and sun," Chuck demanded.

Lori snapped her fingers at the nearby crowd of waiting helpers as she responded. "I've brought a botanist to make sure you have the correct amount of water and other nutrients, Chuck. As for sun, it is still cloudy and expected to remain so for the rest of the day. So, I have arranged for artificial grow lights. They are only prototypes, but I am told that they very closely replicate sunlight. Will that be sufficient?"

Kip and I stared at her, slack-jawed. Even Kip, whose belief in Chuck's humanity and consciousness was absolute, couldn't believe Lori's level of preparation on his behalf. Already a short, stout man was approaching to inspect Chuck--the botanist, I guessed. Other helpers were setting up the grow lights. They were massive things with open wires and tubes running in every direction. It was the kind of clumsy but functional construction that was a sure sign of a prototype design.

"I'd like to hear a story," I said.

"Of course." She snapped her fingers again and helpers were pulling books out of boxes. "I've arranged for a variety of amusements for you while you wait and we arrange for more permanent accommodations. Was there a particular subject you were interested in? I also have a few fiction selections that are currently quite popular."

I waved my hand, dismissing them. I took a half step towards her, the subtle change in position making it a private conversation.

"I did have a particular subject in mind, but your books won't help. I'd like to know your story. Specifically, I'd like to know why a woman of your stunning intelligence follows Daws."

In the next five seconds, she told me her story, but with her eyes, not with words. At my mention of Daws, her eyes flicked to

the Vortex for only a brief instant. Those eyes told me everything I
needed to know.

Worry. Fear. Sadness.

"Ah. So you love him."

Anger. Indignation. Embarrassment.

"That's a yes. Does he love you back?"

Rage. Fire. Sadness.

"And that's a no. I'm so sorry."

Bitterness. Resolve.

"You can choke on your pity, you horrible man!" Muscles
tensing in her slender throat told me she was fighting a lump
there, excess blinking betrayed the fact that she was fighting tears.
She turned and stalked away.

The helpers who had gathered around to do her bidding
watched her go, conflicted as to whether they should follow. Then
they looked back to us.

"And I would like some fruit," announced Kip, refusing to
let the little disturbance rob him of his chance to have a wish
granted by these gathered people and their collection of boxes,
"and something sweet to drink."

The right boxes were found and brought to the front. The
attendants seemed grateful for something to do and they crowded
each other as they all pitched in to arrange our impromptu picnic.
The effect, naturally, was overkill.

A table and chairs were set up right out in the open air. It
was piled with an assortment of food. A wide selection of fruits
answered Kip's request, but there was also a spread of various
breads, sliced meats, and an array of sauces.

Kip dug in with a vengeance. Lori had done her job of
predicting what he would want perfectly. These were all the foods

that a man living in the slums would never have a chance of eating. I was fairly confident that some of the exotic fruits on the table, Kip had never tasted in his entire life.

We spent a lovely twenty minutes there, we happy three. Kip jumped from fruit to fruit, often only taking one bite before moving on to a new one. He would pause occasionally from his fruit tasting to smile at one of the attendants or to cram a sugary pastry into his mouth.

Tratch marched up to us, a dour expression on his face.

"What did you do to Lori?" he demanded. "I've never seen her like this."

Kip pointed accusingly at me. I, of course, pointed at Chuck. Tratch was unamused and focused in on me.

"What did you say to her?"

"It's hardly my fault!" I defended myself. "I only brought up her little crush on Daws and she went all mean on me, called me names and everything!"

"Yes, that would do it. Rough situation there," he nodded. "That's something none of us talk about. I advise you not to mention it again or she might ask me to kill you."

"And would you?" I asked.

His answering smile was chilling.

"How about you, Tratch?" I changed the subject. "What makes a man with your… talents…join up with Daws?"

Tratch pulled up a chair and lounged comfortably, snatching a pastry from the table and talking around a mouthful of flaky crumbs.

"Daws is going to rule this whole planet. You know that, right?" He offered the information casually, as if it truly were common knowledge. I nodded my acceptance of this fact with similar nonchalance.

"That's likely true, but what does that mean for you?" I pressed.

"He promised that when that's done, he'll let me kill someone." He said it in the same easygoing tone. He took another bite of pastry, his eyes challenging me to ask more while he chewed. I accepted the challenge.

"Do you mean one particular person you want to kill, or you'd like a free license to go out killing folk?"

He chuckled at the thought, spraying crumbs from his pastry down his immaculate uniform.

"I can see why Daws says you're such a smart aleck, Phillip. Still, I don't mind playing your little game. The man I want to kill is a scientist who worked for the other side during the war. You see, my whole family went to war. When I signed up as a soldier, my father enlisted as a combat medic. My mother went along as his nurse. That's how they met, you know, in the beginning. He was a doctor, she was a nurse. I imagine they'd always hoped I'd stick with my civilian research job.

"Anyway, their position was overrun and their field hospital was captured. I heard about it too late. All the wounded were taken prisoner along with my parents. Problem was, their soldiers were spread too thin with the new offensive, so they couldn't spare enough to guard the new prisoners or escort them back to the camps, especially with so many wounded.

"So one of their researchers asked to use them as test subjects for his new compound, a variation on the Gury gas. His colonel approved it, the soldiers sealed off the field hospital, and this scientist pumped it full of poisonous gas, taking careful notes and measurements. You know, seeing how long it took for different people to die and such."

It was a horrifying story, but Tratch told it calmly and smoothly, like he was telling a fairy tale, not relating the painful death of his mother and father.

"I managed to hunt down the colonel who gave the permission and killed him before the war was over. I even got quite a few of the soldiers who sealed up the field hospital, but I never could find the researcher whose idea it was."

"And then the war ended," I offered. Tratch nodded as the first flicker of emotion showed on his face and I caught the merest glimpse of his hatred and frustration. He was a hunter who hadn't been able to finish his hunt.

"Anyways," he popped in the last bite of pastry and finished his story. "When Daws has both nations under his thumb, he's promised that this researcher will be found and imprisoned for war crimes."

"And then?" I suspected I already knew. Another chilling smile from Tratch told me I was right.

"And then Daws gets me into the cell where he's being kept and I kill him with my bare hands."

"You're a dark man," Kip said around a mouthful of pink fruit. "Would you really have us go back to war so you can have your revenge?"

Tratch shrugged his shoulders.

"I don't see why not, wars are often fought for less. Though let's be honest, do you really think Daws is going to need a war? He already took over this country with little more than smoke and mirrors."

"But he's just the Commissioner," Kip protested. "The Oligarchy will take him back out of the position once they feel safe. He hasn't taken over the country."

Tratch and I exchanged glances. Both of us knew that Daws was never going to give the power back to the Oligarchy. He would push them and they'd demand that he step down. Then he would escalate the situation, leaking information, showing video footage.

In the end, the people would cast out their Oligarchs, ignore their Senators, and embrace this new glorious hero as their leader. Who would accept leadership from a fat bunch of bureaucrats when they could bask in the glory of their new king? They wouldn't call him a king, of course, but that is what he would be in practice.

When he wasn't answered, Kip pressed harder.

"And you can't claim this was all Daws's doing. This was a magical portal and crazy beast swarms. It's not like he could have done all of this without that happening, and that was completely random. Daws couldn't have planned all of this."

For the last time, Tratch gave his dark smile.

"You have no idea what Daws can plan, Kipland," he rebuked softly. "I'll tell you this, though, this situation has never been out of his control."

Kip snorted derisively.

"Yeah, he looked really in control as he scrambled away from the falling building because his plan to kill all the bugs failed."

Tratch shrugged sheepishly.

"Actually, I guess if I'm being fair, that was my plan. Daws usually leaves the destruction and killing stuff to me."

"I guess we all have our talents," Kip muttered sarcastically.

Chapter 13

*Nearly every old religion has some symbolism tied to fire. I
wonder why...*

–Musings of the Historian

After we had finished our meal, we were ushered toward
one of the neighboring buildings. Rooms had been prepared for us
and we settled down as night fell. Kip tossed and turned for a
while, groaning occasionally around his overfull belly, before
falling asleep. I waited patiently in the dark for the story to pick
up again.

It was late the next morning before the first of the refugees
came stumbling out of the newly constructed building. Their
clothes and stunned expressions marked them as Yrris's people. I
recognized a few of them from my trip through the Vortex.

They clutched small homemade bags to their chests, caught
between fear of the unknown ahead of them and the horrifying
memories of the terrors behind them.

They were greeted by soldiers who directed them to various
areas that had been prepared with food and water.

I stood with Tratch and watched the little procession.

"I wonder how Daws and Yrris are doing," I pondered
aloud.

"Hmm…" mumbled Tratch. "You're right. You'd think they
would have come through first, leading this lot. Excuse me a
moment, would you?"

He hustled off and gathered officers around him. They huddled in conference, occasionally turning and pointing at one building or another. One by one, soldiers would nod or salute, then run off. I didn't know everything about how rank worked in their military, but I was quite certain that almost all of the men Tratch was ordering around outranked him significantly.

Still, they scurried when he directed. It was a known fact that Tratch operated with the authority of Daws. A mere appointment to Commissioner wouldn't have created this dramatic of an effect. These men were already used to jumping when Daws said jump. As I suspected, he was always much more than a colonel.

"Look!" Kip pointed at the line of people coming out of the building. It had been a river of people up to this point, packed tightly and moving quickly. Now suddenly, the river had dried up. No more people followed the last stragglers. The last few people urgently spoke and gestured to the soldiers who greeted them, but the language barrier prevented any real communication.

Still, the soldiers could recognize panic when they saw it and were already hurrying the refugees out of the area while new soldiers filed in, forming into lines and shouldering heavy weapons. Tratch was suddenly at my arm.

"I need you to come translate what these people are saying. They seem awfully excited about something."

We hurried off together towards the soldiers. Most of the refugees were already gone, taken to some other location. A couple remained, however, trying desperately to communicate with the soldiers. I saw them drawing in the dust on the ground and gesturing wildly, though they had given up trying to speak.

"Hello!" I opened. Everyone turned as if all their heads were connected by a single string and I had jerked on it. "Can I be of some assistance?"

"Shriver is coming!" one of them shouted. I didn't recognize him.

"He says Shriver is coming," I translated dutifully to Tratch. I expected him to get frustrated at the useless bit of knowledge, but he only absorbed the information and turned to some of the soldiers that stood around him.

"Single target. Imminent arrival. Suspected fire theme. Get me all available firefighting equipment from the city converging on this location. Have the outer boroughs gather their equipment as well and bring it in closer, but maintain a perimeter of at least two kilometers."

Three of the soldiers saluted and rushed off.

"How did you get the information about the fire?" I asked him. He pointed down to the ground where the leader had been drawing furiously. It was an amorphous shape, but wavy lines ended in jagged points. It was a rough drawing, made in a rush by a poor artist on a crude medium, but it still managed to convey the violence of the flames. "Ah, I see."

"Everyone needs to leave here!" the refugee spokesman urged me, pleading. "They are all too close."

"He says we need to leave and that we're too close," I translated to Tratch. I found that Tratch didn't take himself quite as seriously as Daws, so it wasn't quite as much fun to tease him.

"Ask him how far back we need to be," Tratch prompted. I translated the question.

"There is no safe distance! He will burn us all to ash. If we could pull a mountain on top of us and hide amongst its roots, we still couldn't survive his sustained wrath. Run and keep running!"

"He says Shriver is quite hot and suggests your soldiers move back another fifty paces at least," I offered. Tratch rolled his eyes.

"That was clearly panicked rambling, Phillip. We'll get no more useable intelligence from this one." He waved his hand and soldiers escorted the last few refugees away. Tratch turned to his waiting lieutenants. "Have the men move back fifty paces and establish a new perimeter. You, get in contact with…"

"TRATCH!" Daws roared. "It's right behind us!"

Daws and Yrris staggered out of the building. His soldiers came out after him, walking backwards, weapons pointed back towards the entrance. As they caught up with us, I could catch the distinct smell of smoke and sulfur clinging to them.

"Let's go, people! Move out!" Tratch yelled at the remaining soldiers around them. As a group, we ran for the perimeter. Daws was already briefing Tratch as we ran.

"It was less than a minute behind us. Even with the time difference, it'll be here any second. It's an enormous fire elemental. I don't know how much of it is solid and how much is flame. It's possible it won't even be able to fit through the Vor…"

A loud creaking and roaring behind us drew his attention. We turned to watch the building that had been so expertly and swiftly crafted be torn apart from the inside. The heat of an incredibly intense fire incinerated the bonds that held the outer walls together and they fell outwards, already crumbling as the inferno weakened the bonds that held them together.

As the outer walls fell away, they exposed the inner scaffolding, burned black and twisted to jagged shapes like the burning bones of some prehistoric monster.

"Launch acid." Tratch had gotten a hold of a communicator

and was already issuing orders through it. The roar of the fire drowned out the noise of the launchers, but we could hear the pop as they exploded above the creature and for the second time that day, a burning rain settled over the contested spot of land.

This time, however, the deadly acid had no effect. The falling drizzle flashed and steamed as it came close to the flames, but the deadly monster didn't seem to notice as it finished wrecking the building like a toddler toppling blocks.

"Airbornes ineffective, move the launchers back to beta," Tratch continued his steady stream of orders into the communicator. "Begin volleys."

Around the perimeter, officers shouted orders at their men. It was a testament to the discipline of these soldiers that not a single one of them had yet run away from the enemy confronting them. As the orders were called, they obediently started firing their weapons in a rhythmic pattern into the mass in front of them.

Shriver, the fire elemental, shrugged off the last remnants of the burned building and roared his full bulk into the world. Heat distortions twisted the air to the point where it was hard to make out any distinct shapes in the burning mass. Searing flames seemed to turn back on themselves, constantly pulsing in and out of the central mass, like a sun pulling solar flares back into itself by sheer force of gravity and magnetism.

The volleys of projectiles, streams of fiber pellets that would have ripped a human army into bloody shreds, slammed into the mass of flames. The waves of small arms fire didn't have any effect on the fire elemental, however. Shriver didn't seem like he'd noticed any of the attacks yet.

"Where's Lori?" Daws shouted over the roar.

"She's on her way. She left for a little while last night, but I heard that she was on her way back this morning."

Daws was furious. "Why would she leave at a time like this?"

"It was Phillip's fault, sir," Tratch deflected, uncomfortable bearing the brunt of Daws's fury. The look Daws shot at me would have melted holes in plate steel.

"Well get her here now! Get the men back, they're having no effect and they're still within range of its attacks. Once it's through, it will attack."

"Once it's through?" Kip interjected. I don't know when he had rejoined us, but there he was, Chuck clutched close to him. "It looks like it's through now."

"That's not all of it," Daws shot back, irritated at the interruption. Sure enough, as large as the thing was, it was growing bigger as we spoke. Parts of it moved like muscles, giving the impression of something writhing to squeeze through a small space. Daws's attention turned to Yrris, though he spoke to me.

"Phillip, ask Lady Yrris what she knows about this creature," he ordered. I translated his request directly, feeling too distracted watching the fire elemental unfold itself into this world to do anything else.

"This is Shriver," she spoke quickly, stuttering over her words as she tried to supply as much information as possible in a short amount of time. "He's considered to be one of the most powerful Tanniks, one of the only ones known to have killed other Tanniks in his rage. He's wild and unpredictable, only held in check by one even more powerful.

"He is a recluse and doesn't involve himself in mundane matters like dealing with humans, so we don't know much about him. His presence here can only mean that we've drawn the attention of the First."

I translated a short version for Daws.

"The name is Shriver. He's a mad dog and Yrris is more afraid of the one who let him off his leash, someone called the First. She doesn't know anything that will help you fight him."

It was indicative of how distracted Daws was that he didn't even take the time to chide me on my obviously abbreviated translation. He only nodded and went back to conferring with Tratch.

Behind them, Shriver had filled the space where the building used to be. He also started to take on a more distinct shape. It was vaguely humanoid, but only in the roughest sense, like the drawing of a two year-old.

An arm lashed out, growing longer in an instant and it slammed through a column of soldiers, scattering their charred bodies like fallen leaves.

"We're still too close!" cursed Daws. "Get everybody back, now!"

"FALL BACK! FALL BACK!" Tratch yelled into his communicator. All around us, people were gathering necessary supplies and running away.

As Daws turned to join them, Tratch caught his elbow and leaned in close. I stepped twice, keeping out of their line of sight, but moving in close enough to hear the last of their hurried, private conversation.

"…end it, sir?" Tratch had asked something.

"Not yet," Daws responded. "Let's get these people out of here. How long until the firefighters can get here?"

I couldn't quite make out Tratch's response, but Daws was

unhappy with it.

"Then get thinking about your alternatives. We've gone through acid and projectiles and this thing hasn't flinched. If water doesn't work, you'd better have another plan ready."

Tratch snapped a sharp salute, humbled by the rebuke, and hustled away. Daws whirled on me, almost hitting me as he spun into the confrontation.

"I don't like being spied on, Phillip." His face was so close to mine that I could feel his breath on me and hear his hissed threats over the roar of the fire to the side of us. "I don't know who you are or what you're doing here, but you are only alive because you are useful. Push me too hard and I'll have to rethink that arrangement."

"That's very scary, Mr. Daws, sir," I drawled back in a dramatic whisper, "but you picked the wrong moment if you were trying to be the scariest thing here. I'm going to have to give that title to the raging fire demon to your left. But don't feel bad, I think it's really only a size thing. If you were as big as the assembled flames of a burning forest, you could probably give old Shriver there a run for his money."

I reached out and patted his shoulder reassuringly. He shrugged it off in irritation and started walking away.

"Come on, then!" he shouted back over his shoulder. "I can't have you burned to a crisp yet. I insist on having that pleasure myself!"

Chapter 14

A steady focus can break down and solve any problem, if given enough time.

–Musings of the Historian

In a delicious turn of circumstance, Shriver struck in that moment. Something like a flaming fist slammed down on me, crushing me to the ground. The heat flash boiled my blood and seared the flesh from my bones. I felt all of this happen in less than an instant, but by the end of that same instant, I was whole again, my body unharmed.

In the two full seconds that I was engulfed in flames, the sensations flickered back and forth so quickly that it seemed like both states existed simultaneously. I was horribly burned and mutilated at the same time that I was perfectly fine.

Then the flames were gone and the moment that I was perfectly fine caught and held. I rolled swiftly to the side, coming up stumbling and coughing as hard as I could manage.

"Phillip!" Daws yelled. He was scrambling up himself from where he had dived for cover from the attack. "Are you all right?"

"Yes!" I assured him, interrupting myself with another bout of vigorous coughing for added effect. "I barely got out of the way, though. Had I leapt left instead of right, I'd be roasted right now!"

He beckoned to me furiously and we scrambled away together. As we ran, I looked up, right into the wide eyes of Lori. She was standing a good thirty paces away. Her face was pale with worry at seeing Daws so nearly incinerated, but her eyes were on me.

She had seen. I hadn't gotten out of the way of the attack and she knew it. Now, a battle would be going on in her mind as her logical brain tried to sort out conflicting facts. In five minutes, she would have it explained away, I was certain.

She would convince herself that her depth perception had been off, or there had been a trick played on her eyes by the heat distortion, like a mirage in the desert. It might take some work, but it would happen. That is the tragedy of educated minds. As they grow to understand the mysteries of the universe, they slowly become blind to its wonders.

"Tratch!" Even as he ran, Daws was shouting, working the problem. "What do you have for me?"

"I've got two tankers that can be here within two minutes," Tratch shouted back.

"Two tankers... aren't going to be enough," Daws panted between breaths. It wasn't meant to be heard by anyone, but we were running so close together it would have been hard for me to miss it.

He was right, of course. I had seen the tankers they used for fire control here. It was a large tank of water on wheels with a pump on it.

Their only real hope was the additives that they put in the water. The chemists of this world were first rate, and they had compounds that they put into the water that served to drain the heat and oxygen out of a fire much better than pure water.

Still, if this had been a normal fire, two tankers would have been insufficient, and this was no normal fire.

I tugged on Daws's sleeve and pointed. We pulled up from

104

running and watched the tankers rolling down a parallel street. Men in full heat suits jogged alongside the tankers with weapons in their hands, escorting the massive, slow-moving carts.

Watching the initial attack was like watching a slow lava flow come in contact with the ocean. We waited and watched as the tankers drew up within range of Shriver, who was still raging at everything around him, burning everything left standing in the large patch of devastation surrounding the Vortex.

They were agonizingly slow as they set up their pumps, aimed the streams, set up triggers for the jets, and made their way clear of the tankers before setting them off.

The long wait and military precision paid off, however. Steady streams of water shot almost simultaneously from both tankers and hit Shriver directly in the middle. Dark spots appeared amongst the flames and billows of steam erupted from the collision of water and fire.

"Ah ha!" Tratch exulted, carried away in the moment of seeing his enemy wounded.

His joy was short-lived, however. Shriver turned slowly, noticing the water, but there was no panic or pain in his demeanor. A clumsy arm reached out through the jet of water, not bothering to get out of the way. We could hear the sizzle of steam even from our distant location.

But while the water darkened a spot in the flames, the bright, fiery arms continued to reach out until they grasped the tankers themselves. The fiber concrete construction glowed a moment under the heat before failing, dumping thousands of gallons of water onto the ground, forming a wide, shallow pond between the two tankers.

Then Shriver showed his contempt for the water by placing

a hand directly into the pond. Huge clouds of steam blurred our view of the scene. The image looked like a piece of violent abstract art. Bright colors, dark shadows, and brightly lit steam all mixed together in chaotic glory. No patterns could establish themselves in the rising whirlpool of smoke, flame, and steam.

"Maybe not the best swimmer, but he doesn't seem to fear the water," I quipped. Tratch scowled at me. Daws hung his head.

"We need to move further back. How much of this area have we managed to evacuate?"

"We've got all the buildings cleared for a mile in every direction. Troops were working on it all night." Lori reported. Daws shook his head.

"That's not going to be enough. Tell the troops to start expanding the perimeter immediately."

Tratch was already giving orders into the communicator before Daws had finished his sentence. Daws, meanwhile, turned his full attention on Lori.

"I expect and demand your full attention to this situation, Lori," he fumed. "When I need you, I'd better not hear that you've wandered off. Is that understood?"

"Perfectly, sir!" Lori's every fiber was drawn tight in military rigidity. A clenched jaw was the only thing that betrayed her inner emotions.

"Good. Now analyze. What can we bring against this thing before it destroys everything?"

"It's very big, sir," Lori stated with authoritative finality. Daws and I stared at her, confused. We both had deep respect for Lori's powerful intelligence. Her simplistic observation was rather out of character for her, especially as she stood expectantly, as if she had revealed some great truth and now was waiting for Daws to give orders based on the new intelligence.

"Umm…" Daws started uncertainly. "I'm ready to agree with you, but I'm not seeing the relevance yet."

"It's too big, sir," Lori supplied helpfully. Her jaw was relaxed now, and her eyes weren't quite as hard. It wasn't quite a smirk or a wink, but I understood now what was going on. She had been shamed by his rebuke, now she was asserting her own self-esteem again, showing how much he still needed her.

"Are you saying it's a weakness? Can we use its size against it?" Daws fumbled for the answers. Lori shook her head, finally relenting and giving us the full explanation.

"It's too big to fit through the portal, sir. We also haven't seen it actually lift or push anything with its flame arms, it only burns things where they are. Combine these evidences and we must conclude that Shriver is not the flames themselves, he only controls them. Shriver himself must be small enough to fit through the portal."

"Excellent!" Tratch beamed from the side. "That means we just need to harm the core."

Tratch's mind, as always, was on tactics and destruction, and seeing his enemy as something manageable had lifted his spirits after the crushing defeat with the water attack. Off to the side, Shriver was already starting to move. He moved slowly, ponderously. Luckily, he wasn't heading toward us. He left behind the charred wreckage of everything the military had left in their panicked retreat. Now he moved towards the largest concentration of buildings to continue his incredible show of force.

"Would enough water work, then?" Daws asked. "Penetrate to the core, whatever it is, and cool it there? Or perhaps a big enough volley of projectiles could hit the core, at least by accident..."

Lori was shaking her head.

"It's too big, sir. We've already seen that the heat is enough to break down our fibers, so projectiles would likely turn to dust before they reached the core. As for water, we've seen that it doesn't worry much about it. It wasn't able to penetrate the flames much at all. We'd never get close to the core."

Daws grumbled in frustration and started pacing.

Kip pulled Chuck in closer and moved a little to the left, effectively hiding behind me. With all the rage coming from Daws, Kip and Chuck seemed to be doing their very best not to be noticed at all. They remembered all too well when Daws had almost used them as test subjects with the Vortex.

"Lori!" Daws rounded on her in fury. "I need a move here. Tell me everything you can surmise or guess about this creature."

"Umm..." Lori started slowly, cowed a little by the sudden aggressive questioning. "It shows intelligence, so there must be some sort of brain or neural network in there. But the components couldn't be what we're used to..."

Her eyes lit up and her rambling focused as her mind caught on to the idea.

"Any intelligence needs cells, and cells need to be fed," she talked faster and faster as her mouth tried to keep up with her brain. "Normally, blood or other fluids feed the cells, but this thing couldn't use anything water-based. Still, it would need to be liquid, so it must be some sort of molten metal or salt that it uses."

"Go on," Daws urged.

"So there has to be something similar to our bodies, solid and liquid parts. The liquid is going to be molten, and the solids

108

would have to be something that had an even higher melting point than the liquids. Sir, it would have to be a delicate balance."

Daws finally jumped in on the conversation, starting to see the possibilities.

"How does cold kill a cell?" he asked, musing.

"The water inside freezes, forming sharp crystals that expand and shred the cell wall."

"Would it do the same thing if the liquid were something not water based?"

"No, sir. Water is fairly unique in the way it expands when it freezes. Most other liquids contract. So even if we could cool it down a little, it might not actually destroy the cooled cells, they could, theoretically, continue functioning as soon as they heated back up. We can assume from the massive amount of energy here that they would reheat almost instantly."

"So even if we could get water to the core, it would heal itself." Daws spoke more to himself than anyone else. Then his head rose and an odd light filled his eyes.

"Lori, how does heat kill a cell?"

"Heat kills a cell in a variety of ways. It breaks down the proteins in the cell. Even if the proteins didn't cook, the water would expand or even turn to steam and burst the cell from the inside."

"And how would that apply to cells with molten metal fluids?"

"The same way!" Lori exclaimed excitedly. "Even if it managed to avoid boiling, the additional heat expansion would still strain or burst whatever material it uses for cell walls."

"Then we burn Shriver."

Chapter 15

Physics and reason; both seem to break down at the extremes.
　　　　　　　　-Musings of the Historian

"Tratch, do we have any napalm stations still operational?"

"Yes, sir! All of the launchers to the south managed to pull back far enough before Shriver got to them. Now he's heading north, so they're safe."

"Perfect. Get them moved into position and commence firing."

"Yes, sir." Tratch turned to his communicator and started issuing orders. Daws turned back to Lori.

"Will napalm be enough?"

"It's possible, sir," she hedged. "But it's not very likely. His own flames are at least as hot as our napalm, so he'll be prepared to handle that level of heat."

"So it's useless?" Daws asked.

"No, sir. If Shriver isn't flexible with his heat generation, then our napalm will prevent him from dispersing enough heat. In essence, if we keep his own flames in with our own and keep him from cooling off, his own heat might burn him from the inside. It's worth a shot. I only mean we should be figuring out our next step."

"Naturally," Daws agreed. "So how do we make fire hotter?"

"Well sir, fire has three components, fuel, air, and heat. If we…"

"Sir, a couple of our stations report that Shriver is still in range for their launchers without any repositioning. Shall I give the order?" Tratch held the communicator ready, casting an apologetic glance towards Lori for interrupting her discourse on fire.

"Have them wait for a count of one hundred," Daws commanded after thinking a moment. "Then have the two of them start firing in a staggered pattern. I want a steady rain of napalm, not just one big blast."

Tratch turned to his communicator to relay the orders, and Daws turned to us.

"Come with me, I want to see what effect it has. Lori, start counting to a hundred."

And just like that, we were jogging right back down the path we had been running away on only ten minutes before. Shriver had moved far enough away that a building blocked our view. Luckily, we didn't have to move far before we were clear of the building and we got a clear view of Shriver as he was moving away, tearing through another building.

There was a childish joy in the way he tore into the structure. Clumsy arms and legs beat and kicked at the buildings playfully.

"88…89…90…" Lori panted right beside us. Of our little group, she was having the hardest time with all the running around. While every bit of her demeanor proclaimed military precision, she clearly didn't maintain the military standard of fitness.

I suppose that isn't completely fair--there was one member of our party who was doing a little worse. Chuck, still clasped tightly in Kip's arms, was looking incredibly ragged after the

111

vigorous jostling. Kip ran with a rhythmic military jog, reverting to his bygone training. The bouncy gait shook even more dirt out of Chuck's pot, which already had some cracks from its recent trip down the side of a building.

Lori must have been counting a little fast, because she had reached "112" before we heard the distinct "PFFT" sound of the launchers. True to their orders, one launch followed another in a perfectly timed sequence. Napalm rained down on Shriver with the regularity of a heartbeat.

The first few launches landed with no effect at all. Shriver didn't notice the extra heat at first; he continued thrashing at the offending building. As the assault continued, however, the flaming behemoth paused. Various sections of the writhing flames pulsed. It was like he was checking himself over, looking for malfunctions.

He came to the realization suddenly and spun like a fiery tornado. He didn't have noticeable eyes, as his head was just another amorphous glob of flame, but his entire frame jerked back and forth, searching. Then he saw the napalm, which was raining down on top of him.

The counterattack was swift and brutal. Screams of men reached us as all the launchers were attacked simultaneously. Shriver grew shorter by half in the blink of an eye, shooting outwards from the bottom like a collapsing column of water. The launcher teams, suddenly too close to Shriver, were washed away in the infernal flood.

We were close enough to feel the heat and we scattered backward, tripping over each other as we reacted to the sudden wash of flames.

"Fall back!" Daws gasped as we scrambled back to our feet.

The order was largely unnecessary. We were already headed back the way we came, quickly putting a building between us and Shriver.

Tratch led the group, running back to where he had left his communicator. This world hadn't quite figured out wireless communication yet, so even with the vast military resources at play here, there were still limitations to how far you could move from established networks.

"Everything's quiet," Tratch reported. "I can't be sure without visual confirmation, but I believe all launcher teams have been lost."

Daws accepted the information stoically. None of us had expected anything different.

"Are we safe here?"

"Lookouts are reporting that Shriver is still raging where we left him. We are out of range, as far as we know, but not by much. Still, we've seen that it takes him time to move through a building, and at this location, there are two buildings between us and him."

"Very well, we'll hold here for a moment and reassess..."

"Sir, you've got a call," Tratch interrupted, his face looked grave. "It's the Minister."

"Ah yes, I suppose that was inevitable. Are we ready?"

Tratch nodded and handed the handset over. What followed was half a conversation as all of us tried desperately to hear what the Minister was saying without looking like we were trying to eavesdrop. A hand tugged at my sleeve.

"What's happening?" Yrris pleaded. "Are we defeated? I saw the attack on Shriver failed. Is there nothing that can be done now? Why is everyone so concerned about this latest report?"

"Calm yourself, Lady," I reassured her. "This is far from

over. What you saw back there was not a battle, but a test. The test was ultimately successful. Once Lori applies her mind to it, the puzzle will be solved and Shriver will fall."

"Then why is everyone so tense right now?" Yrris pressed.

"They're not tense about Shriver, they're tense about the leaders of the nation. They will have been getting reports and the fear will start to get at them. They'll want control of the country back."

"They would take command away from Daws for one minor defeat?" Yrris asked. "But he's done so well so far."

"Oh, they absolutely would," I replied. "They're operating on fear alone. Imagine you're in a dark room full of dangerous weapons and you're trying to find your way out. If your outstretched hand hit a sharp edge, you'd pull back sharply and go a different way, wouldn't you?"

"Of course," she affirmed.

"Well, these leaders are the same way. They are way out of their depth and struggling to find their way out. A loss is the same as a sharp edge in the dark. It hurts and the fear takes over, telling them they're going in the wrong direction."

"So will Daws still help us after he's lost power?"

"Daws isn't losing power," I chuckled outright. "The leaders have imagined power, built on the foundation of tradition and societal momentum. In short, they're in charge because they're in charge. Daws has built real power, wielding love and hate on either hand."

I gestured towards Lori and Tratch in turn as I mentioned these two powerful forces.

"On that foundation he has also built fear and respect. The leaders of this land have misunderstood power and have only doomed themselves by trying to match their imagined power against Daws's genuine article. One will break against the other like spun glass against an iron ball."

Behind me, I heard Daws responding to an obvious tirade from the Minister.

"I understand your concerns, Minister, and I share them. However, I haven't heard from the General so far, so I won't be able to consult with him, as you've suggested. In my mind, your own safety is key and I'm not sure your current location is far away enough from possible danger. My men will escort you to a better location. Travel safely, Minister."

Daws ended the call even as small noises from the handset suggested the Minister still yelling on the other end. He handed the communicator back to Tratch.

"See to it that our Oligarchs are well taken care of, Tratch," he ordered. Tratch accepted the communicator and went right back to work issuing orders to distant forces.

"That's it," I whispered to Yrris. "That's likely the last time anyone will see the nation's leaders."

"Good!" Yrris made it sound like a curse. "If they are so frightened and weak, they are not fit to lead the nation during a crisis like this."

"Sir," Tratch spoke up. "There's been a bit of a problem. Oligarch Nelson had a communicator of her own. She's been talking with some of the other generals and they're forming an opposition."

Irritation flared across Daws's face and he swore under his breath.

"Get our men in there immediately. Put a stop to this," he ordered tersely.

"They're already there, sir, but Nelson had some of her own guards who are causing some trouble in the transition."

"This is starting to fall apart," Daws mumbled, running his hands through his hair. "I don't have time for this, I need to deal with Shriver. Authorize deadly force, Tratch. I can't handle this diplomatically anymore."

"Yes, sir." Tratch saluted sharply and went back to his communicator.

It was an incredible escalation. Right in the middle of this raging battle with the Tanniks, Daws had started a civil war on the side. If Oligarch Nelson had a communicator, then it stood to reason that she would get word out before the last of her bodyguards were taken down.

Loyalties would be tested. Those who remained true to the old government would be coming hard for Daws. He had managed to place himself squarely in the middle of two wars. Not bad for a single day. There was something in my Historian heart that loved him for that. I still didn't like him as a person, but I grudgingly had to give him my respect.

People like that changed the course of history itself. Sometimes they were good, more often they were evil, but the events they set into motion became the foundation of legends.

It has always puzzled me how few people try to make big changes in the world because they think that one person can't have that great of an impact. However, every history book on every world is crammed full of names, not of organizations or causes, but of people. Those people were the ones who introduced ideas, invented new things, and even toppled regimes. Even more remarkable is the fact that they often did it starting from nothing.

To change history, a person must first and foremost believe

that they can. It is a circular kind of logic that somehow keeps most people from ever trying. So it falls to people like Daws and Lady Yrris.

Chapter 16

Power demands a fine line. Those without power becomes slaves,
whether they recognize it or not. Those with power risk enslaving
others, whether they recognize it or not.

–Musings of the Historian

"He looks upset," Lady Yrris observed.

"Yes, the old government is not going to slip away as quietly
as he had hoped. He's been able to fight this war with the full
support of the military up to this point, but now many of them are
going to become his enemies. You could see soldiers killing
soldiers before this evening is done."

"Humans killing humans?" Yrris was outraged. "We have
seen such things from the rage-crazed or the insane, but to start
an entire war amongst yourselves? Surely it is madness. Why have
soldiers if you're going to have them shoot other soldiers?"

"It's horrifying, to be sure, but the people here don't have
the Tanniks to kill them. So, logic follows that they must kill each
other."

"What kind of dark logic is that?" she demanded. "Are
people such savages in your eyes? Are you saying that if my
people didn't have the Tanniks to fear we'd turn on each other?
What a dim view of humanity you must have, Phillip."

"Not dim at all, milady," I explained as Daws and Tratch
took turns on the communicator in the background. "And it is not
man's savagery that leads to war. Rage or hate might lead to a

118

killing, that's true, but war is something much larger and actually tied to a nobler motive."

"Noble? Now I'm sure you're toying with me, Phillip." She scolded. "How could something as awful as war be tied to anything noble?"

"Quite simple, and I would never toy with you, Lady. I just see things a little differently than most. It comes with age. The fact is that people crave the company of other human beings. We band together and form bonds of warmth, love, compassion, and mutual protection.

"As populations get bigger, this instinct pulls them into larger and tighter groups. Soon, the concentration of people overwhelms what the land can support. This creates a feeling of scarcity."

Yrris jumped in, interrupting me. "But surely they could find more resources. The world is a huge place."

"It's true that they could," I agreed. "But I didn't say real scarcity, I said the feeling of scarcity. That feeling makes people afraid and they retreat even deeper into their group. That's about the time they start coming up with names for their group, and other names for other groups. The feeling of scarcity makes them feel that it's 'us or them.'

"Whether it's months, years, or decades after that, it hardly matters. The groups are going to war. But you see that it's not about anger or even hate, though of course those develop. It's actually a kind of misguided loyalty, a devotion to one's own people that starts making people look at others as an enemy."

Yrris paused, thinking through what I had said. To her credit, she didn't immediately argue back. She took the time to understand. I was even more impressed by what she came up with next.

"Do you think the Tanniks are the same? Are they loyal to each other and we are the enemy?"

"I think it says a lot about you that you are able to empathize with an enemy that has been so cruel to your people. To answer your question, though, I doubt that it's the same for the Tanniks. I have my suspicions that they started out much the same as everyone, feeling the same scarcity and that must have driven them for a while.

"But what I see before me now has nothing to do with scarcity or loyalty to one's own tribe. This is power unchecked. I have seen those that seek for power above all else. Sooner or later they figure out how to trade pieces of their humanity for more power. They make trade after trade until they are flush with power, but have lost all of their humanity. Don't you agree, Lori?"

Lori jumped, startled. She had been standing nearby, ostensibly guarding us as Tratch and Daws were otherwise occupied. Kip and Chuck had needed no guarding. Both were sitting in the dust, happy for the chance to rest, even though Shriver was marauding a few buildings over and civil war was erupting only a few paces away.

So she had left them and sidled over to where Yrris and I were talking. She had maintained a respectful distance, looking off into space while holding herself in a stiff-backed military parade rest. Still, her head had moved slightly, unconscious adjustments to help her hear better as our conversation got quieter.

"I don't know what you mean," she dismissed my question. I pressed her.

"I think you do. You worry about him, don't you? Now,

now, don't get upset. I'm only saying that you've been closer to him than anyone on this path. It would have been completely unavoidable. He's had those chances to trade his humanity for power. What did he choose?"

"Daws is a great man!" she professed vehemently. "It's easy for small minds like you to sit back and question him, but you don't know what he's been through, all the people he's helped."

"A beautiful answer," I remarked. "Though it didn't really match my question, did it?"

She blushed, but said nothing more.

"That's what I thought. Both you ladies might take a moment to consider the path that would turn a man into a Tannik."

Both flinched. Fire flashed in Lori's eyes and she opened her mouth to defend Daws, but she was interrupted by the man himself.

"We've got to move. A couple of our lookouts in key positions aren't reporting to us anymore, which leaves holes in our intelligence. We can't be sure of Shriver's path at the moment, so we'd better get some distance."

We gathered what few items we had amongst us and moved out, heading directly away from where we'd last seen Shriver.

The layers of calm control were peeling away from Daws like bark from a burning tree.

"Tratch!" he snapped. "Who controls the Vortex?"

"We do!" Tratch eagerly supplied the good news. "Though it's not uncontested. General Hines has men on the way and our own men were severely depleted in the initial attack by Shriver."

"General Hines?" Daws smiled. "He's the one leading the

opposition? At last some good news. Bring in more men, I don't want to lose the Vortex."

"They're already on their way, but Hines is going to get there first."

Tratch hesitated, weighing his options and wondering if he dared question his commander.

"Sir, it's not the best location to be playing a defensive role. The structures we had up were all thoroughly destroyed and the rubble is still too hot to clear. We can set up a perimeter around the Vortex farther out, but we'd be spread thin and easy pickings for shooters who could fire at us from the cover of the surrounding buildings and wreckage."

Daws's jaw clenched, the muscles in his face working as he struggled to contain his frustration.

"You're right, Tratch," he admitted. "Not even Hines could miss that kind of opportunity. Have the men surrounding the Vortex fall back. Have them move some of the bodies from the dead launcher teams into their positions, though. We wouldn't want Hines to know we gave up the position willingly. Let him think us weak."

Tratch smiled broadly, relieved to see that logic had triumphed in Daws's mind. Far too many commanders would make reckless decisions when things got emotional. Now Daws had confirmed Tratch's faith in him. As angry as he was at the new developments, he wasn't going to spend his men's lives cheaply.

"Pull everyone back to the tertiary location. We'll meet them there."

The tertiary location turned out to be an operations base that Tratch's men had set up in one of the evacuated buildings east of the Vortex. We walked into the building past guards and rooms of materials and weapons that had been stockpiled there. If the area surrounding the Vortex could be considered the "front lines," then this building was the forward supply depot.

I watched with great interest as the soldiers reacted to our entrance. Emotions flickered over their faces, changing from one to the other from one blink to the next. They became more serious as they saw Tratch--the man inspired fear and discipline. However, they stood taller as they saw Daws. He inspired something more. I knew then why these men had been chosen to guard this important location. They were believers.

Their eyes passed over Kip, Chuck, and me with little interest. We were clearly refugees, and the only thing they might be curious about was why we were being allowed to accompany Daws during such extreme circumstances.

Their eyes then landed on Yrris. Her noble bearing and clearly foreign appearance inspired curiosity and suspicion. By this point, every man there knew that they were at war with alien powers, so the appearance of someone who was clearly alien would undoubtedly be the cause for much discussion once we'd passed by.

Finally we made our way to a makeshift command room that had been set up. Our core team filed in and sank gratefully into padded chairs that had been placed around a low table. Daws didn't waste any time.

"Tratch, do we have eyes on the Vortex?"

"Yes, sir," Tratch reported. "Hines' men have already taken up position guarding it and they're starting to put together scaffolding for a new temporary building."

"What's happening now?" Yrris whispered at my shoulder.

123

"A general supporting the original government has taken control of the Vortex."

"Why does that matter?" Yrris asked. "Shriver is already through. He won't try to go back. He will continue destroying everything in sight until he's stopped, there's nothing left, or the First calls him back."

"And which of those do you think is most likely?" I asked.

"Shriver destroying everything," she growled bitterly. "Daws wasn't able to stop him with the entire might of this world at his disposal. Now you're telling me that he's going to have to fight his own people. So I don't see how they can stop Shriver now."

"And what about the First calling him back?" I pushed further, not bothering to address her lack of faith. "Any chance of that happening?"

"I doubt it." She was already shaking her head. "I'm shocked that the First took any notice at all. Entire generations have passed without him making any sort of appearance. Most of what we know of him is from legends, though my grandfather saw him once."

"Is he really so powerful?"

"Oh yes. My people live under the rule of the Tanniks. They are like gods to us, though cruel and oppressive. If the Tanniks themselves have a god, it's the First. He will occasionally interfere in their affairs, but humans are too low a species for him to take notice. Daws takes more interest in the condition of Chuck the plant than the First notices our people. And for that we are grateful."

I nodded and turned my head to look at the developments around the table. I ran right into the staring eyes of Daws. He peered at me with deep suspicion, even as he was listening to Lori give her assessment of their situation. He waved a hand and she stopped speaking, her report put on hold.

"Phillip, would you care to share with us what you were talking about with our guest?" The question was polite enough, but his voice held an edge. With failures racking up against him and opposition forming, he was beginning to see enemies everywhere.

Chapter 17

Anyone who says it can't get any worse lacks imagination.
                    -Musings of the Historian

"Certainly, sir, Commissioner, sir!" I responded, my tone an over-enthusiastic parody of everyone else's willingness to obey. "The lady and I were discussing your chances of victory under the current circumstances."

Daws looked toward Lady Yrris for confirmation, knowing that she also would have understood my words. She looked away, embarrassed, and Daws had all the confirmation he needed. He looked back to me.

"And how do the two of you see my chances?" he asked coldly.

"Sir, we are divided on that point. She thinks you've all but lost already. With a divided country, she thinks it's only a matter of time before Shriver reduces you all to ashes."

I threw it in his face to provoke a reaction, but he only nodded. If anything, I thought I saw the hint of a smile play at the corner of his lips.

"And what do you think, Phillip?"

"Me?"

"Yes, you. I'd like to hear your opinion." He had downshifted in mood and was oddly earnest. I could find no reason behind the change, and when confused, I tend to turn to honesty.

"I think Shriver and Hines have no idea what they're up against. Shriver's a bully and a child, destroying because it's fun. Hines is old and like many old men, clings to what he knows. Neither motivation is going to be strong enough when pitted against the hunger festering in your soul."

Again, Daws surprised me by not reacting to my words. He nodded again, thanked me for my honesty, and turned to Kip.

"How about you, Kip? What do you think about our chances?"

The ex-soldier straightened a little in his chair. This had been a harrowing ordeal, full of terror and violence, but Kip had responded surprisingly well. I saw a bit more of the reasons why now. He had lived a long time in that slum, lost in his delusions and pain. Now he felt important. It hadn't healed his mind or eased his pain, but now he felt like he mattered and it was putting some iron back in his core.

"Honestly, it doesn't matter much whether we win or lose. Some people are going to survive and some are going to die. This is a war, and we're going to fight, that's who we are. This nation has been defeated before in history, but we've never surrendered. I don't believe we'll start now."

"Well spoken, Kip," Daws nodded. "And what does Chuck think?"

As usual, I couldn't quite tell if he was being sarcastic, trying to keep Kip happy, or was sincerely covering all options. As usual, Chuck answered in Kip's voice.

"We're all going to die!" he wailed. "Haven't you been paying attention?! These things are magic. There's been swarms and fire and Phillip is over here talking to the pretty lady about much worse. The only hope left is that they'll only kill off you humans and leave the plants alone!"

"We can hope," Daws's mask of respectful concern never faltered for a moment. He turned to Lori and saw her answer in her eyes. She was his, whether he wanted her or not. It was a reckless, foolish kind of love. It has always fascinated me how often such things struck among the logical and highly educated. It's almost as if the more they push every other part of their lives into tidy little boxes, the more a wild part of them thrashes and yearns for something uncontrollable.

"Tratch, did you want to weigh in?" Daws asked. Tratch's roguish smile told all of us his answer. He was having the time of his life.

"Sir, this is the best fight you've ever brought me. I wouldn't miss it for the world."

In many ways, Tratch was like a big game hunter, always trying to find something more dangerous and rare to bring down. It was a primal sort of dominance for a primal sort of man. Bringing down the Tanniks would be a thrill like nothing this world could have ever offered him.

Though he claimed revenge as his motivation for joining Daws, I doubted he would have left anyway. It was the true loyalty of someone who enjoyed his work.

"Phillip, kindly tell Lady Yrris that we've discussed the issue among the group and each of us has found some form of hope in the current situation. Advise her to do the same."

I turned to do so, but Daws suddenly motioned with his hand for me to be quiet. His head tilted to the side as if trying to catch some elusive sound. We all fell silent and listened as well.

"Tratch?" he asked in the silence. "Did we not order our soldiers to not engage with General Hines and his men?"

"We did, sir," Tratch affirmed.

"Then why do I hear sounds of battle?"

Now that we knew what we were listening for, it became much clearer. Our ears had fooled us in` had been close to us, soldiers moving boxes, dropping things in other rooms, things like that. Now, with direction, everything fell into place and we could hear the sound of launchers in the distance.

"I don't think that's our men, sir," Tratch responded. "Could Hines be attacking Shriver already?"

"Not a chance," Daws shook his head. "The sounds are far too close and Hines is far too careful to jump in without extensive plans and backup."

As if it had been waiting for its big moment to jump into the conversation, the communicator in Tratch's hand chirped to life and he held it up to his ear, mumbling little updates as he heard them, though his focus was clearly elsewhere.

"Something is coming through the Vortex... Hines' men are being pushed back... Some kind of intense wind... Launcher teams being thrown around like paper... Initial attacks don't seem to be having any effect... Both acid and napalm ineffectual..."

He continued to issue steady reports in the background, but Daws had already wheeled on me and Lady Yrris.

"Ask her what she knows about a Tannik using wind."

"Lady, they're reporting strong winds throwing things and people around. Do you know what's coming?"

Her shoulders sank even further, her body language suggesting someone cringing from a beating.

"It's Shawen," the name came out like a sob. "She is the air Tannik. We have never seen a limit to her power, she is considered second only to the First himself. Her presence here confirms that the First has taken an active interest in this world."

"The name is Shawen," I reported dutifully to Daws. "She's an air Tannik and second in power only to the First."

"I'll need to hear more about this 'First' very soon, but ask her to tell us more about Shawen for now. Why has she come?"

I translated and Yrris supplied her best theory.

"This is an invasion. Shawen could destroy the city faster and more thoroughly than Shriver ever could, but that's not her style. She has a deep hatred for mankind. The First keeps her far from the slaves, as her appetite for killing is insatiable. Death sought for intimidation and control. Shawen wants us destroyed.

"It's clear now what the First intends. He has sent Shriver through to draw our attention and to wreak havoc through the city, driving people into scared groups. Now Shawen is here to shred through the population. I can only imagine her joy at being unleashed."

Daws's face grew dark as I translated this new information.

"Gather the soldiers, Tratch," he ordered. "I would see this for myself."

Lori opened her mouth to question the wisdom of such an action, but thought better of it as she saw the hard set of his jaw. Tratch did not share her reservations and was already jabbering into the communicator, even as he opened the door and shouted to the gathered guards there. They scampered away at his command, scattering to find and gather their fellow soldiers.

With flawless military efficiency, our honor guard assembled around us as we exited the building. Other squads of soldiers formed up with us, jogging in perfect cadence as they drew in from their various locations.

I was surprised to see the size of Daws's army as it

assembled. We had only ever seen certain soldiers as they had come and gone. I knew that Tratch had been coordinating attacks with squads around the area, but I hadn't realized how many there were.

Tratch had called them all in. Yrris' report had told him that Shawen would hunt and kill them all if she could. Whether or not we'd be any safer as a group wasn't certain, but Tratch was getting into fight mode now. Like a warrior strapping on sword and shield, he wanted his forces ready to hand.

The assembled battalion filled the square and overflowed into surrounding neighborhoods. Supply carts were passing up and down the lines and quartermasters were passing out side arms. They were the same weapon that Daws carried at his waist, bulky, lacking elegance, but versatile and deadly.

Daws had claimed the design was a prototype, but he had clearly been much further along in the production process. And even though the soldiers handled the weapons with a certain sense of awe, they did not act surprised or unfamiliar with the new armaments.

They had seen these before, likely trained with them. Daws had been ready for war, building his own private army right under the noses of the government, it was only natural that they would be better armed and better trained than the country's rank and file troops.

"Move out!" Tratch roared, chopping his right hand in the air, fingers extended, to give them direction. Our main little party walked at the head of the vast column.

For all their size, the army moved with surprising stealth. At one point, Kip looked back to check that they were indeed still following. Our journey was a short one. We hadn't been stationed very far from the Vortex to begin with, and now the perimeter surrounding the area was even larger.

Our first contact was with other soldiers, who were running, scrambling, and sometimes screaming as they fled the horrors behind them. Silently, soldiers from our own contingent folded around these fleeing soldiers, silencing them and tying them before leaving them in doorways. We didn't have time to manage prisoners at the moment, so such distractions could only be dealt with swiftly and left for a later time.

We formed up at the outer edge of what had become a substantial clearing in the midst of the city. Several buildings were down now, and violent forces had pushed them all outward from the Vortex. So we had ample rubble to provide cover as we peeked over and around edges at the slow massacre taking place in front of us.

The last pocket of soldiers was trapped up against one of the last standing buildings in the area. All military discipline was gone and it was a teeming mass of panic. Problem was, none of them had anywhere to go.

Any soldier that tried to escape was either flipped high in the air and allowed to fall to his death on the rubble, or crushed to the ground under the enormous pressure of winds that acted like a giant hand smashing the life out of a bug.

Shawen was taking her time, enjoying the experience, feeding off the fear like some kind of psychological parasite. Most of the soldiers had accepted that flight was out of the question and cowered pitifully, awaiting their final end.

"There's Hines," Tratch whispered to Daws, pointing to a man cowering with the other doomed soldiers. He was on his stomach peeking over the rubble, Daws was next to him, and I had positioned myself on the left side, convenient for eavesdropping. As they spoke, another soldier was tossed several stories and allowed to drop. Tratch shuddered.

"That's no kind of death for a soldier," he muttered. "Should we do something? We could likely draw its attention long enough to let them get away."

Daws didn't respond right away. It seemed like an eternity as he weighed his options. Two more men died as he considered.

"There's nothing we can do." He finally uttered his decision like he was pronouncing a death sentence on his rival. It was a fitting tone; Daws knew what he was doing.

"Yes, sir," Tratch said. It was the first time I'd ever seen him reluctant to follow one of Daws's orders.

Chapter 18

War, defense, law, and even mercy occasionally require killing. It is unavoidable in these fallen worlds. But anyone who enjoys it is a monster.

-Musings of the Historian

It was a sickening sight and yet not a single person could bring himself to look away. If it had been some romantic epic, Hines would have been last, probably after rallying his men to one final act of defiance. Instead, he met a rather anticlimactic end as he huddled with his men. Rank was forgotten as horror brought them all to the same level of chilling mortality.

Shawen treated him no differently than she had treated the others. When it was his turn, he was plucked from the crowd like a petal from a wilting flower and tossed high into the air. Whatever loyalty, love, or stories he carried with him died ignominiously as his screams were cut short.

The slaughter continued as Shawen played with her new distractions. There was a deep cruelty to her actions that made me feel cold inside. I tore my eyes away to look at Daws's soldiers as they crouched under cover, watching men wearing their same uniform get methodically executed.

As expected, horror was splashed across their faces. Many of them cringed as each new man was taken and killed. However, there was another emotion running through the crowd if a person knew where to look. It was relief. As horrifying as the scene was,

134

there was definitely that little voice in their heads telling them to be happy it wasn't them.

I did not doubt their courage. This hand-picked band of men would undoubtedly charge and attack fearlessly should the order come, but there was something about the way they molded themselves into the rubble that spoke of reluctance to even be there. It was as if they were trying to seep right into the pile of rubble and disappear. I couldn't blame them.

Shawen was hard to define. Shriver had made the effort to form his fiery apparition into a vaguely humanoid appearance, arms and legs. Shawen had no such compulsions. She was the condensation of a hurricane.

The air whipped around unpredictably, swirling and lashing at ground and rubble. Slabs of concrete that would have taken heavy duty cranes to move into position were tossed around like dry leaves. The closer you got to the center of the maelstrom, the more intense the winds became. The ground immediately around the center was clean, anything that could be blown away had been blown away.

Directly at the center, the flows of air became so fast and focused that they looked like a spider's egg cocoon and emitted a steady roar like a powerful engine.

"She's in there," Yrris offered, pointing towards the white tangle of air at the center of the windstorm. I nodded. It was an obvious fact, but like everyone, Yrris was feeling the need to do something, anything. Even Daws wasn't immune to the impulse. He turned to Lori, trying to make use of the first-hand information.

"Analyze, please, Lori." He had to say it twice before she cleared her throat and made a feeble attempt at unraveling the mystery in front of her.

"It will undoubtedly be a complete slaughter, sir. There's no escape route and it appears they've stopped trying. The sounds we heard earlier suggest that all available armaments have already been tried. Look there, there's evidence of both napalm and acidic launchers. They clearly had no effect."

"What about Shawen herself? What can you tell me? What am I not seeing, Lori?" Daws pressed fervently. Lori was one of his greatest assets, and right now she was spiraling, emotions overwhelming her cognitive abilities.

"Even that doesn't make sense, sir." She was almost sobbing and I realized that she was also struggling with all the apparent breaks in the laws of physics. "All the air seems to be pressing outward, that's why nothing can get to her. That shouldn't be possible! Air has to come from somewhere. Matter can't just be created. It has to be coming from somewhere, and the first person to say anything about magic is going to get a fist in the mouth!"

Daws seemed almost grateful for the distraction, a problem he could deal with. He patiently guided Lori's mind away from the frustrated panic that threatened to overwhelm her mind.

"You're absolutely right. You've been right about everything so far." He calmed her with words with the same tenderness of a parent stroking the head of an injured child. "Others have dismissed these things as magic, but you've managed to discern the reasons underneath this whole time.

"I want you to take another look. If this is still tied to the laws of science you understand, then there will be a hole somewhere. Tell me what doesn't fit in this situation, please."

The final "please" did wonders to bring her back from hysteria. She wiped an errant tear from her cheek and forced herself to look back at where Shawen was continuing to pick off survivors. Gone was the hanging jaw and held breath. She looked over the situation with clear eyes, determined not to let Daws down.

"She's on the ground!" she exclaimed triumphantly. Soldiers nearby looked at her with horrified expressions, worried that the sudden loud noise would draw the attention of the Tannik, but Shawen remained focused on her current victims. Only ten remained. Our time was limited.

Daws nodded encouragingly. "Yes, she is. What does that mean?"

"If this were all magic, wouldn't you expect the 'Air Tannik' to be riding the winds, an embodiment of the air itself? Or if the air were truly pressing outward in all directions, she would be suspended in the air. Instead, the center is clearly on the ground."

"Yes, yes, go on!" Daws urged. Eight survivors remained.

"And look at her primary attack. Throwing people into the air. She can push them down, but only for tiny fractions of time. Mostly she pushes up or out. That tells me she has to push off the ground, action and counteraction. It's basic physics, sir, if you're going to push…"

"Lori…" Impatience was starting to seep into Daws's voice. Five survivors remained. "I need something I can use. Quickly."

"Sorry, sir," Lori blushed and cut to the root of the matter. "She's going to be vulnerable from below."

Two survivors remained. Daws grinned. He turned to Tratch to work on tactics.

Tratch's eyes were still fixed on the last survivor. He was a nameless soldier, numb and limp from the trauma of the last half hour. When his body fell, he didn't even scream.

"Everyone down! Pass the word," Daws hissed at his men on both sides. The word passed like wildfire and before Shawen had turned from her grisly work, Daws's army had disappeared below cover.

"Tratch, she's vulnerable from below. What can you do with that?"

Now that the spectacle was done, Tratch focused again on what he was good at.

"The most important part of any trap is making it look normal," Tratch mused. Like Lori, Daws gave him the time to reach his conclusion. "If we break up any of the concrete here, it's going to be noticeable. We also don't have much time for digging, so something that already has some sort of underground work being done would be optimal. Do we have any way of directing where she goes?"

"Phillip, ask Lady Yrris if there's any way of influencing Shawen's movements."

Lady Yrris was already at my elbow and perked up at hearing her name. She was the only one of our party who hadn't been shocked or appalled at Shawen's display of cruelty. That was the world she had come from. For her, this hadn't been traumatic, only a reminder of what she was trying to escape.

"Is there any way of luring Shawen into a trap?" I asked. She nodded somberly.

"She hates my people in particular. If she sees any Argothians, especially here, away from the controlling influence of the First, she will pursue them no matter what."

"Do you know what you're saying?" I asked her.

"Yes, Phillip, I do. When I discussed this with my people, we knew that there was a chance that we'd have to fight, and die, for

138

the opportunity to live free. I don't even have to ask them, they've already agreed before I stepped through the Vortex."

I turned to report to Daws...

...and couldn't.

My voice locked in my throat and I felt a familiar compulsion. It came as a bit of a shock after I'd had so much freedom to participate in the story up to that point. Now my interference was being stopped. That could only mean one thing. I turned back to Yrris.

"I'm sorry, Lady, but I can't translate your words this time. It would change the story."

"What?!" Daws hissed, almost at my ear. "What nonsense is this? I need that information right now. You do your job or so help me I will see you sacrificed to this creature! Don't you understand how many people could die right now if you don't help? Or do you just not care?"

"I care," I responded simply and calmly, a perfect balance to his fury. "But it's not a choice for me. It would be like trying to push yourself from the ground with two broken arms. I can't change the story, and telling you what she said would change the story."

He snatched his sidearm from his belt and pointed it at my face. He opened his mouth to issue his threat, but found no fear in my eyes. Worse, as he looked deeply into my eyes, searching for something he could use, he found himself getting confused. He blinked and turned away.

"Sir, are you all right?" Lori placed a hand on his arm and glared at me suspiciously.

"I'm fine," he growled through gritted teeth. "Just running a little hot is all. Do we have anything we can use to compel Phillip to cooperation?"

She shook her head. "I fear any threat that could produce immediate results would be so extreme that he would likely suspect us to be bluffing. Then, once we proved that we weren't bluffing, we would have already destroyed whatever leverage point we were threatening to begin with."

Daws groaned and gripped one hand in his hair, actually pulling some loose in his frustration. Something about seeing Daws like that brought out the pettiness in me and I smiled to see him so uncomfortable.

"Fine. Please keep a closer eye on Phillip and let's try to figure out some sort of long-term leverage." Daws glanced toward where Kip huddled amongst the debris, clutching Chuck to his chest. "Maybe a plant of his own, eh?"

I chuckled generously at his little joke, it was the least I could do. Still, in my own thoughts, things were getting exciting. Up to this point, everything had been set. I'd been able to participate in the story all I wanted, because in the end, my contributions weren't actually going to change the outcome.

Now that Yrris had suggested bringing her own people into the fray, it was a true turning point. Granted, she had only suggested using them as human bait, but the fact that I was stopped from interfering suggested that there was a much greater impact.

"Lori, work with Yrris. From the way she's glaring at Phillip, she also knows he won't be helping this time. See if you can't work out what she was trying to say."

"Yes, sir," Lori responded and crawled over to where Yrris was already smoothing out a patch of dirt to help illustrate her thoughts, should gestures and expressions fall short.

"Tratch," Daws began. "What are we seeing from Shawen? Do we need to relocate?"

"No, sir. She seems to be following after Shriver, probably trying to find the people who were driven out of the buildings he's destroying. If what we've heard before was true, then time was going a lot faster on the other side of the portal.

"So Shriver and Shawen likely intended to come together, one right after the other. The time delay meant that Shawen came through hours after Shriver, even though she probably only waited a short while on her side before coming through.

"It's a two-pronged invasion. Shriver is clearly meant for shock and intimidation, attacking buildings and infrastructure. They would rightly assume that such destruction would drive people into groups, either as refugees or to coordinate a defense.

"Then Shawen comes through like an anti-personnel bomb, shredding through the population, breaking through whatever resistance had started to gather against Shriver. It's genius, sir. It's what I would have done."

It was high praise coming from Tratch, who considered his own tactical and strategic genius the standard by which all others should be measured. Daws nodded his agreement.

"Phillip said that Yrris had mentioned someone called the First a few times. He must be the brains behind this. While powerful, these Tanniks have leaned on brute force. I don't see them planning this out with such detail."

"Agreed, sir. Shawen is the real attack, Shriver is here as a setup. I recommend we focus on destroying her first. If we manage to take her down, Shriver may very well retreat."

Chapter 19

The instinct for survival is primal and overpowering. That is what makes self-sacrifice such an incredibly powerful gesture.
                                    –Musings of the Historian

Daws had been nodding along, but at this last statement, he stopped, his jaw flexing, and leaned in towards Tratch, though he didn't bother to whisper. Rather, his voice got louder as his emotions raged under the smooth surface of his face.

"I don't want Shriver to retreat back through the Vortex. I want him dead on our soil. I want him crushed for the whole world, both worlds, to see. Do you understand?"

"Perfectly, sir!" The gleam in Tratch's eyes was wolfish and hungry. It was a focused hatred that drove Tratch, and Daws had wielded it like a surgical laser. Now he would use it like a war hammer.

"For now, we'll focus on Shawen. Can we get ahead of her and plant a trap?"

Tratch shook his head.

"We'll need time to get it set up. If we miss it the first time, she'll be on guard and I doubt we'll get another chance. Getting that far ahead of her on her current path would run us right into Shriver, and we're not ready to take him on yet."

."Phillip," Daws's tone showed how much he resented needing me in that moment. "Could you please ask Lady Yrris if we might expect other Tanniks through the Vortex?"

"I'll try," I offered. "There's more at work here than you know."

"Lady Yrris." I pulled her attention from where she had been drawing figures in the dust, pointing towards Shawen in the distance, then drawing other figures and pointing towards herself. She turned.

"Daws would like to know about any other Tanniks that might be coming through the Vortex."

She thought it over for a moment, then shook her head.

"Most of the other Tanniks embody other magics that make them too large to come through the portal. They are beasts, mountains, or metal giants. Even those couple who might be able to make it through would not dare risk getting in the way of Shriver. It's no accident that the First sent Shawen; she is possibly the only one so powerful that she need not fear Shriver's flames."

I turned back to Daws and both of us were surprised when I was able to deliver the translation without so much as a stutter slowing me down.

"She says this is probably it. The other Tanniks are either too big to come through or they're afraid of Shriver, who has something of a reputation as a Tannik killer."

He nodded gratefully.

"Any chance you'd be willing now to tell me what Lady Yrris told you earlier?"

I opened my mouth to try, but again hit a wall.

"No, I'm afraid not. Still, I saw them working it out over there. I imagine you'll have the answer on your own soon."

"And you won't stop them from telling me?" Daws asked suspiciously. "Is the secret less valuable if someone else tells it?"

I shook my head.

"There's a lot you don't understand, Daws. This isn't about secrets, this is about stories. This isn't my story, so there's a limit to what I can do within it."

His next question surprised me.

"Where is your story? Can I help you get back to it?"

I was shocked at the concern in his voice. Then my memory kicked back in and I remembered what he had said earlier. He was looking for leverage, something that I wanted that he could use to secure my cooperation. I sighed.

"If you could do that, I would conquer both worlds and present them to you on a silver platter. Sadly for both of us, that's well out of reach."

"Are you insane, Phillip?" The question wasn't a jab or insult. It wasn't even asked rhetorically. He was asking me in true sincerity. I was touched by the honesty and responded in kind.

"I'm not sure, but I think so."

His nod was a short bow of gratitude as he sensed the truth of what I had said.

"Is there any way I can control you?" Again, an honest question. So again, an honest answer.

"Neither the magic of the Tanniks, nor the combined technologies of your world, nor your will, nor even my own, will keep me from my path."

We were moving again. As I expected, Yrris and Lori had managed to communicate the plan entirely on their own. They smiled and hugged one another as they finally achieved their goal. I wondered what would have been different if I had voiced her entire plan. From my own perspective, I could see no change in the story, except possibly the budding friendship between Yrris and Lori.

144

Maybe that would mean something later on.

Now we were rushing to the abandoned building that had been hastily converted to a refugee camp. The conversion had mostly consisted of knocking down walls to create a much larger public area, and sealing off most of the doors to make the building easier to guard.

We burst into the common area like a hammer strike. The people jumped back in alarm, then surged forward as one when they saw Yrris. They thronged her like a savior. Tears ran freely down her face to see them. For the first minute or so, no words were spoken. It was a sacred moment of gratitude to see one another safe amid the turmoils raging around them. Even Daws did not interrupt.

Finally, Yrris drew herself up tall, the reaching hands pulled back, and all fell silent, sensing the gravity of the moment.

"Death has fallen." None reacted to this incredible news and I guessed that she had already told them this when she went through the Vortex to gather them. So it wasn't said as something new, rather, she was subtlety reminding them that the impossible had already been done once. It was visibly effective as several sets of eyes switched to Daws with looks of admiration and awe.

"But now Shriver and Shawen have come through, looking for us." This news had a much more substantial effect. Gasps rippled through the crowd like a wave, and chatter broke out everywhere. Yrris silenced them again with a raised hand. She spoke with confidence and hope, which I recognized was a show put on for her people. The last I had spoken with her, she still felt that their course was a suicide mission.

"Daws and his men have powerful magics that can hurt Shawen," she announced, and hope pumped smiles and tears into the crowd. "But they need our help. These magics take preparations, and can only happen in a specific location. While they prepare their attack against Shawen, we need to lure her to their ambush."

The room burst into noise. A few were shouting arguments against the plan, but they were a weak minority. Some were bravely volunteering themselves to die. Others, more serious in their dedication, were only asking where Shawen was now and where she needed to be led.

While Yrris discussed details and offered comfort and answers, Daws edged his way over to me.

"What are they saying?"

"The usual stuff. Daws is a powerful wizard but he needs the blood of babies to assume his ultimate form, things like that."

"Right," Daws rolled his eyes. "And how has the crowd responded? Anyone offering up their babies?"

"Indeed they are. As you can see, the mothers are a little more hesitant, but the men seem willing enough. That group of older men there are the fathers of teenage children. They are asking if it has to be babies, specifically, or if any young person will do."

Daws growled his displeasure at my flippant attitude.

"I see brave men stepping up to sacrifice their lives in defense of their families. Can you really treat their courage so irreverently?" he asked.

"I treat everything irreverently," I responded. "It's really the only way to be fair, you see."

"I see," he said drily. "Is there anything you take seriously?"

"Well," I drawled as I winked at him. "There was this girl…"

He rolled his eyes again and moved back to talk to Tratch,

so his back was turned when my smile faded.

Now Yrris had waved Lori over with her maps. They were already depending on me less as their visual aids got more advanced. Lori was able to indicate places on the map, using nearby landmarks to establish reference, then using small figures and drawings to show the locations of Shawen and Shriver. Yrris also helped explain things as Lori demonstrated the plan in miniature. The two made a good team.

It was more risky for Yrris and her people than it needed to be. Several passable locations had been pointed out that would be somewhat closer to Shawen. However, the final decision was made to pick the best spot possible, even though it meant that Yrris and her people would have to lead the Tannik on a much longer chase.

Tratch had been the one to suggest the perfect spot. It was a park that was having new utilities run through it, so all the construction and excavation equipment was already in place. Even better, much of the park already had an extensive sewer system running underneath it.

It would be an easy job for Tratch and his men to seal off the large pipes, then drain them, creating large empty spaces beneath the park that they could fill with explosives, poisons and acids.

Tratch was feeling freer than ever, feeding off of Daws's anger. He was becoming ever more inventive in his lust for destruction. Regardless of whether they won or lost, the park would have to be quarantined as a dangerous area for years to come.

That was the first time that I discovered that Tratch hadn't actually been a battlefield commander during the war, nor had he remained a regular soldier after the war ended.

Rather, he had worked in the research department, coming up with new methods of destruction. Daws had been directly involved in several of the projects, often as Tratch's immediate supervisor.

While Tratch's technical knowledge had often been lacking, Daws had become impressed with the way Tratch thought, as he often put things together in sequence to maximize the destructive effect.

Daws had taken him under his wing and introduced him to some battle training simulations. Tratch's strategic genius had only increased when faced with multiple variables. While they had come quite a ways since the lab, Daws and Tratch obviously still had ready access to the latest innovations coming out of the war labs.

Now here in a tranquil park, all the state-of-the-art compounds were cleverly concealed, waiting for detonation. There hadn't been a good way to train Yrris' people to avoid triggers, so in the end it was decided that Tratch and his lieutenants would trigger the traps personally.

From our observations, Shawen didn't move much faster than a normal person, so we were optimistic that Yrris and her people would be able to stay ahead of Shawen, while still staying close enough to keep her interest, until they hit the park. Once they had crossed the park, the people were supposed to head straight to a building on the far side that would keep them safe from the blast. It was also upwind, so there would be little risk of chemical fallout poisoning them.

Lori had gone with Yrris and her chosen band. Kip and Chuck had also elected to go with them. I was a bit worried at that development, as Kip wasn't the best runner, but he wouldn't be deterred. He had shown that he could be at least as fast as Lori over short distances. It was his endurance that worried me.

Now Daws, Tratch, and I were climbing the stairs of the tallest building overlooking the park. It would give us a good vantage point so Tratch could be more accurate in his detonations.

Tratch had to put a shoulder into the door to break it loose. There had been some water damage and the door had swollen slightly, sealing itself into the frame. Tratch threw himself against the door three times before it burst outward and the three of us staggered out onto the flat roof, looking around to see if Shawen was in view yet.

To our horror, she was already much, much closer than we had expected, and moving faster than we had thought her capable.

Chapter 20

Some decisions come down to what you can live with and what you can't.

-Musings of the Historian

"That's faster than a person can run," Tratch noted and turned quickly to his work of getting his communicator plugged into the network. With those seven words, he voiced our worst fear. Even if they had begun with a significant head start, Yrris' people would not have been able to keep ahead of Shawen all the way to the park.

Our fears were confirmed as the first of the runners broke free of the line of buildings and ran for the park, stumbling for the force of winds that already nipped at their heels. Worst of all, there were much less of them than there should have been. I saw Lady Yrris, recognizable even from a distance, stoop to help someone to their feet who had stumbled. They were towards the back of the pack and in imminent danger.

Daws swore bitterly under his breath.

"It looks like the slaughter has already begun. At this rate, they won't even make it through the park. Is there anything we can do to slow her down?"

Tratch looked pained.

"We could have some of our men break cover and fire on Shawen, but that would only be risking their lives. We've seen that our weapons are completely useless against her. Worse, it

150

would alert her to the possibility of ambush. We've only got one shot at this, sir."

The growl started low in Daws's throat until it erupted in a frustrated roar. Daws threw a map of the charge placements, the only thing he had available in his hand, to the ground and stomped on it. Then he made a decision and rounded on Tratch.

"Have the men break cover and provide suppressing fire."

Tratch knew better than to question his commander in a moment of extreme agitation and parroted the command into his communicator.

Far below us, men that looked little bigger than ants from our lofty vantage points sprang out from bushes, ditches, and abandoned buildings. They all had their weapons out, pointing at Shawen. I couldn't hear the discharge from that distance or over the growing roar of wind, but a sudden flare in the intensity of the air currents around Shawen showed that she had noticed the new threat.

As hoped, she drew up, halting her pursuit of Yrris and her people while she assessed her new enemy. As expected, none of the small weapons fire seemed to do much of anything to Shawen. She lashed out at the nearest teams.

To their credit, they didn't break formation. Instead they beat a hasty, but orderly retreat back toward the park, but at a different angle, so as to keep Shawen away from Yrris and the other runners. As Shawen started to follow them, the teams on the other side of the park rushed in, increasing their attack and trying to draw the Tannik's attention.

The technique worked and Shawen turned from one prey to another. The hunted team used the same circumspect path to retreat, trying to draw Shawen further into the park. If they couldn't get her into position directly, maybe they could do it in angles.

Having switched roles, the first team now became the hunters, pushing at Shawen's back, trying to gain her attention again. It was a dangerous kind of game. I could only admire from afar the incredible bravery and presence of Daws's soldiers. It was like mice taunting a tiger.

Shawen was not to be lured away a third time, however. She stayed focused on the second team, gaining on them swiftly. The first soldier came within range of her elemental force and was swatted like a fly against a building by a blast of air. He fell and didn't rise again.

The other soldiers were retreating in earnest now. They still held a semblance of formation, but they were scrambling away as fast as they could go.

It wasn't fast enough.

Three more soldiers fell within her range and were swept aside like so many blades of grass before a scythe.

"I'm going down there," Daws said, even as he turned and ran back toward the stairwell we had just exited. Tratch swore and followed. Just to fit in, I also swore and scampered after.

Our trip down the stairs took less than a minute, but eternities had passed back on the square.

In the time it took us to descend the many flights of stairs, the second squadron had been completely wiped out. Their bodies lay strewn along their path of retreat like broken toys. Shawen roared over them. As much as a pure elemental force can express emotion, she seemed exultant.

Now, her attention shifted to the other players in her little game of chase. Yrris and what was left of her original team had made the far side of the park, right where they should have been if the original plan had held.

The problem was that the original plan was now in tatters. The soldiers who had given their lives to save Yrris had led Shawen too far to the side of the park. If she pursued the bait now, it would take her across a corner of the park, but she wouldn't ever be on top of any of the major charges.

The rest of the people had continued running, headed to the safe house. They had endured horrors to bring Shawen this far. They would now leave it to Daws and his magics.

Only Yrris turned to watch. She turned and locked eyes with Daws from across the park. He pointed furiously to the center, shaking his head as hard as he could, trying to communicate that the plan was about to fail.

It was shaky communication, but somehow she got his general meaning. Without a second thought, she got her feet moving again under her and was sprinting back to the center of the park.

"Confound it!" Daws realized his mistake too late. He had been indicating the position of the trap, but Yrris had taken it as an indication of where she needed to go. Now she would be standing directly on top of the trap meant for Shawen. He waved and tried to get her attention, but to no avail. She was now focused on Shawen.

"I should have beckoned her to us," he said to no one in particular, Tratch was connecting his communicator again. "We're standing in the perfect position."

Yrris now stood at the center of the park, human bait in the jaws of our trap. She yelled her defiance at Shawen, using her own magic to swirl the air around her. It was a pathetic display

153

when contrasted to the raw majesty of Shawen's power, but it was a clear challenge from one air sorcerer to another.

Shawen, whether noting the challenge, recognizing Yrris, or simply because Yrris was the next closest target, started moving towards the small, defiant woman.

"Tratch, I hope you see your moment." Daws uttered the words like a prayer before battle and burst into a run towards Yrris. I breathed in deeply the smell and taste of that moment. It was a pure and beautiful moment, the kind that usually only happens once in a great story.

There was Shawen, a violent, roiling disruption of nature itself, pure power and cruelty bearing down on its next victim. There was Yrris, a noble slave using her last free breaths to shout defiance at her executioner. And there was Daws, an ambitious, ruthless force of his own, abandoning his schemes and calculations to risk his life to save another.

Such moments have fed my heart through dark years.

Sadly, there wasn't much hope for a triumphant ending to this one. Yrris was standing directly over the primary trap. Tratch had done an incredible job planning this one, even though some of the setup had to be done with improvised materials.

Hundreds of pounds of explosives rested calmly over vats of corrosive liquid and under crates of extra tools they had found nearby. The directed blast would launch the tools upward through the ground, a red-hot storm of shrapnel stabbing up from below. Then, should Shawen survive that, she would be falling back into a vast crater, molded by the explosion, that would be coated and damp with slimy chemicals that would dissolve bone and flesh instantly upon contact.

Such a trap laid and executed against enemy soldiers in

wartime would have had Tratch executed for war crimes, but in this case, all rules had been discarded in this scramble to survive.

Daws was surprisingly fast, but Shawen had seen him now and was increasing speed herself. Wind was already whipping at the two people as Daws grabbed Yrris' hand and yanked her into a scrambling retreat back to our location.

I sidled up next to Tratch.

"Tratch, I hope you see your moment," I echoed the sentiment Daws had left him with.

"I hope so too," he responded and lifted his communicator to his mouth. From my own perspective, it was clearly hopeless. Shawen had entered the trap zone, but Daws and Yrris were still within the projected blast radius.

Worse, Shawen was right on top of them now. Even if Tratch waited for Daws and Yrris to get clear, they weren't going to make it. Tratch would have to detonate with Daws standing right on top of his deadliest trap.

A single bead of sweat on his forehead was the only sign of any stress in Tratch. His jaw was set, his eyes were steady, and his voice was calm as he talked into his communicator.

"Ready charges. Starting count. Detonate zones Beta and Delta on two, Alpha on four, Gamma on seven...

"One...

"Two..."

Explosions rocked the park, but not where I had expected. I knew that Tratch's men had been setting up secondary traps around the area. It had been understood that if Shawen survived or escaped the main blast, they would need other options quickly.

On the far side of the park, where other exits led away from the main square, secondary traps exploded harmlessly, throwing dirt and rock into the air.

Shawen paused in her pursuit and the air cocoon around her shifted, as if looking backward.

Yrris and Daws scrambled faster away, getting close now.

Tratch continued his steady count as if oblivious to the explosions.

"Three..."

Shawen roared like the fury of a mountain storm and started to head back the way she had come. She recognized the trap now. Showing significant intelligence, she was actually heading towards the site of the explosions, figuring that those spots had already been detonated and would likely now be safe.

"Four..."

It felt like the dirt beneath me punched the soles of my feet. The sound, light, and chaos all happened at the same time. The ground beneath Shawen erupted like a volcano, spewing dirt and tools like weapons-fire, up and through her protective cocoon of wind. Red fire and brown dirt mixed in an inferno marked by oddly bright spots of lights. It was like seeing falling stars set against a backdrop of some infernal underworld.

Whether Yrris and Daws tripped as the ground jumped or they were thrown to the ground by the blast was uncertain, but they sprawled in the dirt, barely clear of the main blast. No attempt was made to get back up and continue running. They covered their heads, curled into the fetal position, and made no extra moves as rocks and dirt fell around and on top of them.

"Five..."

The count continued steady as dirt and rubble swirled and settled. A blurry silhouette started to form near the back of the blast zone. It looked almost like a lost child staggering in the

156

explosion.

"Six…"

Some of the dirt and dust swirled more meaningfully around the dark figure. It was a weak comparison to the awesome power displayed earlier, but Shawen was alive and moving away.

"Seven."

The count ended on seven and a third, smaller explosion erupted right under Shawen's feet. It was a simple charge, no extra embellishments, but the perfect placement of the charge appeared to do more damage than the larger one had, it being slightly off-center.

In a satisfying kind of balance, Shawen was thrown high in the air by the charge, hanging for one fraction of an instant before falling hard to the ground, then lying still.

Chapter 21

War follows the warrior, even in peace.

-Musings of the Historian

Tratch and I were already running forward towards where Daws and Yrris lay on the ground. There was motion in the dust as Daws started to move. Yrris followed suit seconds later.

"Sir!" Tratch's calm finally broke under the emotions of the moment. "Sir, are you alright?"

When we were within a few paces, Daws groaned, then growled.

"Is it dead?" Daws rose on shaky feet, rocks and dirt falling off of him. A cut over his eye bled freely, tracking bright red paths through the thick dirt caking his face. He looked like an undead specter, come to claim Shawen for his own dark kingdom below.

"I think so," Tratch reported, though he looked nervously toward the spot where Shawen's body had landed. If there had been so must as a dust swirl pop up near her body, I'm certain that Tratch and his soldiers would have unleashed an entire volley on the spot.

"Show me," Daws rasped. His voice broke and he doubled over in a racking cough. He first leaned down and helped pull Yrris to her feet.

"Are you alright?" I asked her. She shook her head and had a bout of coughing of her own before she could answer me.

"I hurt everywhere. It feels like my insides are shredded."

I nodded.

"Explosions are always much worse than you'd expect," I lectured. "The shock waves bruise the internal organs. You could have slight internal bleeding in dozens of places throughout your body. Even if there's no apparent injury, you could be months recovering."

"Thanks for the encouragement," she drawled sarcastically. She opened her mouth to comment further, but Daws had already grabbed her arm and was dragging her along with him.

Our bedraggled party took a long route around the main crater. Odd smells and eerie sizzling noises emanated from the pit. Tratch had chosen his setup carefully. The explosive charge had been carefully directed upward so none of the chemicals had been blown into the air.

He had also chosen his chemicals specifically for weight and viscosity. Unlike some chemicals, they didn't vaporize easily and float on the breeze. Rather, they sat heavy and oily on the bottom of the pit. There was splattering on the sides, but as far as I could tell, none of the noxious substances had breached the rim.

Daws leaned on Tratch and Yrris clung to my arm and we worked our way over to where Shawen had fallen.

The body was twisted and broken in too many places to have died from the fall. The explosives had done their job well and what was left of Shawen more resembled a bloody rag than a human being.

Still, a human being she was. The face was drawn and parched, like a mummy. She looked older than any person could be, her joints swollen and her bones brittle. She looked so frail in death that it was difficult to connect the image of this old woman to the air Tannik that had slaughtered all in her path.

"Phillip," Daws's voice had cleared a great deal, though it was still raspy from all the coughing and the dust and dirt he had inhaled. "Tell Lady Yrris to get her people, all of them. Bring them here to witness the great Shawen."

I translated his commands exactly to Yrris and she smiled through her pain and started to turn to obey his commands. He caught her by the arm and stopped her.

"Where is Lori?" It showed his state of mind that he didn't bother with the translation. He asked the question directly to Yrris, a sudden panic seeping into his voice. Yrris also didn't bother to wait for the translation, she recognized the name and her eyes teared up. She shook her head and looked to her feet.

This wasn't good enough for Daws. He gripped her arm tighter, his fingers digging into her arm painfully and she winced at the sudden pressure.

"WHERE IS SHE?" he demanded, giving her a little shake. Daws had made it abundantly clear to Lori that he had no feelings for her, but she would have thrilled to see his desperation now, even if it could be explained as a general losing his key advantage in the middle of a battle. "Phillip, make her understand."

"I think she understands, but I'll do what I can. Yrris, you need to tell me exactly what happened to Lori. While you're at it, I'd like to hear what happened to Kip and Chuck."

The Lady launched into her story like a tortured war prisoner revealing secrets.

"She was so fast," she began. "So much faster than we thought. We ran hard and fast, but after we had passed a couple buildings, she was nearly on top of us. I was running towards the back with Kip, who was the slowest runner. I figured I had to do something or we would both die, so I grabbed his blasted plant

160

from him and threw it through the highest window I could reach.

"He panicked and ran into the building after it and we ran on, leaving him behind. I don't know if he was caught and killed."

I held my hand up to pause her narrative while I passed the information on to Daws.

"Shawen was right on top of them, so she threw Chuck through a window to get Kip to chase after it. She doesn't know if it was enough to save him."

"I didn't ask about Kipland and the plant," Daws growled. The sentiment needed no translation and Yrris jumped into the next round of her narrative.

"Lori was running toward the front of the group, but she was out of breath. Someone to the side of her tripped and they both went down. Something happened to her ankle and she couldn't get up. She waved us on. I tried to stop and help and she pushed me away and yelled something at me. I'm so, so sorry. We left her."

I translated, "Lori tripped and hurt her ankle. She made the rest of them leave her behind."

Daws cursed, but continued his questioning.

"Did anyone see her die?"

"No, we were running for our lives," Yrris shook her head after I'd translated for her. Daws grunted in satisfaction.

I was hesitant to share in his optimism, any encounter with Shawen would be a fatal one. Still, I understood how he was thinking. Lori was brilliant. Only a fool would count her out early.

"Tratch, gather a squad of soldiers and head back along the path, see if you can find Lori," Daws ordered and was shocked when Tratch smiled and shook his head.

"I don't think that will be necessary, sir. Look," he

responded, pointing back over Daws's shoulder. Daws spun on his heel, reeling a moment as he taxed his injured body with the sudden movement.

There, back where Shawen's path had broken the line of buildings, Lori staggered forward, leaning heavily on Kip. Our own tattered group hustled toward them. Yrris had forgotten about the order to gather her people, but I could see them coming out on their own from the safe house. The final defeat of Shawen would be a story told for ages.

Instead, the four of us closed on the lost members of our party. It was a pathetic sight. Lori looked awful. The tight bun was gone and her hair was dirty and bedraggled. Her clothes were ripped and scuffed. More than that, her entire body, face included, seemed to be smeared with a foul-smelling mix of decaying leaves and mud. Dirty water still ran down her legs, leaving dripping footprints behind her.

She was using Kip as a crutch, which worked well, as Lori was a little tall and Kip was a little short. Of course, beyond offering her his shoulder to lean on, he was doing nothing else to support her, so it was an awkward affair.

Both of Kip's hands were occupied holding Chuck. The pot had broken from its trip through the window, and Kip now used a shard of it to hold what dirt he could around the bared roots. He sobbed openly as he held his plant together, his fingers trying to hold the soil in like he was trying to stop the blood flowing from the wound of a dear friend. Each trickle of dirt slipping through his fingers brought on a fresh deluge of tears.

"Please, oh please, oh please," he was mumbling under his breath. I don't think he'd even noticed our presence yet. Even in the midst of my joy at seeing everyone alive and well, my heart

162

still broke a little for him.

The emotions were too real, too intense even for his delusion. Somehow I knew in that moment that he wasn't seeing Chuck the talking plant.

This was a tragic memory playing out for him, some past experience triggered by the trauma come back to haunt his present. I could see in my mind's eye a younger Kip, carrying a wounded soldier, trying to stop the blood somehow. Right in front of me, I could see the desperate helplessness he must have felt as his efforts proved useless and his friend slipped away from him.

I wondered only for an instant if I was the only one touched by Kip's suffering, but that idea was quickly dispelled as Daws groaned next to me.

"Kip... for the love of... Tratch, would you please see to the blasted plant?" Daws ordered, taking his arm from around Tratch, freeing his lieutenant to see to the wounded autotroph. Then he drew himself up to his full height, only wincing once as his wounded muscles and organs protested.

"Lori, I'm glad to see you're all right." For Daws, it was the equivalent of a tearful hug. There would be no show of emotion to give her false hope. Luckily for Lori, there was someone else available to supply a more emotional greeting. Yrris left leaning on my arm to limp over to Lori. Tears streamed freely down her cheeks as she moved to embrace the other woman.

"Forgive me," Yrris begged as she held Lori and wept. Lori looked to me for clarity.

"She feels bad for leaving you behind," I offered. To my surprise, Lori, who had shown almost no regular emotions up to this point, also teared up and hugged Yrris back.

I jumped in and helped support Lori as our little party

163

started back toward the site of the ambush. Tratch and Kip peeled off towards the closest abandoned building to find some pot to put Chuck in. Kip was already calming down, having found someone to take care of Chuck for him. Lori started filling us in on the details of her survival. The story was a short one.

"I saw a storm drain nearby and managed to cram myself into it. It was tighter and deeper than I had thought. I feel quite confident the thing hadn't been cleaned since it was installed." She shuddered a little at the memory and the continuing, clinging smell of decaying organic matter. She continued.

"Shawen passed by shortly after and luckily didn't notice me. But then I was stuck in that drain. I couldn't get myself turned around in the small space. Luckily, a short time after, I heard Kip crying his eyes out over that plant of his. I called for help and he managed to extricate me. We moved more quickly than I thought. He was pretty determined to get Chuck 'medical help.'"

I chuckled and she laughed out loud at the absurdity of the situation.

"You know," she joked. "I only hope that someday, someone will love me as much as Kip loves that plant!"

She laughed again, right up until she made eye contact with Daws. Then the laughter silenced and everything became painfully awkward. I smiled at the human interaction. It was refreshing to have people concerned about regular human emotions again.

Chapter 22

A man who can inspire, can rule.

–Musings of the Historian

There was already a substantial crowd surrounding the dead body of Shawen. Yrris' people stood in shock, not even daring to believe that such a dominating power could actually be swept aside so easily.

The soldiers who had gathered were significantly more celebratory, exchanging stories and jubilant shouts. These were men who had risked charges of treason to follow Daws. This victory vindicated their decision. They had bet on the right horse and they were drunk with the feeling of their own power and immortality, even as many of their fellow soldiers lay dead on the outer boundaries of the park.

The crowd parted as Daws approached. Both peoples had their own way of showing their respect and admiration. The soldiers saluted, a sharp clap of the hand to the chest. Yrris' people bowed as they moved out of his way.

Daws grit his teeth and forced himself to walk without a limp to the center of the crowd, to where Shawen lay lifeless. The crowd gasped involuntarily as he placed his foot firmly on Shawen's face, pushing it more firmly into the soft soil beneath.

"Phillip, if you'll actually translate directly for me, I'll owe you a favor," he offered. I nodded my agreement. I couldn't see the benefit of having him owe me a favor, as I would disappear once the story was done, but I couldn't see the harm of a simple translation, either.

"This old woman came here to hurt us," he began. "She abandoned humanity to become a monster. She thought herself powerful as she killed those who couldn't fight back. If we hadn't stopped her, she would have slaughtered all of us."

Yrris' people nodded their agreement as that last part was translated.

"These Tanniks have forgotten the true strength of humanity. They have underestimated our innovation and cooperation. In their arrogance, they have dismissed us as slaves and filth to be swept from our own streets!"

Daws was yelling now, so I also yelled, providing a true translation, as promised, as I tried to mimic his passion and anger. Celebration was forgotten and soldiers growled anger at the Tanniks.

"We have taught them a hard lesson here today. This was their strongest, their champion!"

He paused and gestured down, drawing attention to the dead Tannik now literally under his foot.

"See what she is now! Where is her arrogance? Where is her strength? Where is that will that would have had us exterminated like rats?! It... is... GONE!" Daws roared. "Her strength was nothing compared to our combined will. Her arrogance could not match our bonds of friendship. Her cruelty could not match our heroism!"

The cheering had begun, throaty and primal. These people were under a unique spell. They belonged to Daws now, body and soul. I felt a little guilty being such a close part of it, even as I roared my own translation. But I took comfort in the fact that I was still meeting no resistance, as I had when I tried to translate Yrris' offer of sacrifice.

For good or evil, the story was still set. With or without me, these people would have pledged themselves to Daws; or there was the darker option: that with or without me, none of them would survive long enough to change the story.

Daws felt the momentum building and stoked the fire.

"These Tanniks are an active threat to our world, and I will not rest until that threat is eliminated! The brave men and women who serve with me know that I will stop at nothing to see our beloved nation safe and secure."

His soldiers roared their agreement and approval. Even Yrris' people cheered, though they hadn't known Daws for more than a day at this point. Daws raised his hand and the crowd fell silent, suddenly cowed by the somber look on his face.

"But is it enough?" he asked quietly. Even after I had translated his words, he waited while the people thought through what he might mean. When they had stewed long enough, he continued.

"Is it enough to secure our own borders? To bury the Vortex under thick concrete and pretend this never happened?

"These brave people," Daws swept his hand outward, encompassing Lady Yrris and the Argothians, "were willing to die to help us. What thanks would we give these heroes? In many ways, they are even braver than we are, for they have lived their entire lives under the crushing thumb of the Tanniks. Our friends have lived, worked, and died as nothing better than cattle!"

His soldiers growled again in anger. One day ago, they hadn't known these people had even existed, but now they had fought together, lost friends together, and now shared both a common enemy and a common hero. Suddenly, the thought of their humiliation at the hands of the Tanniks was galling indeed.

"I've asked so much of all of you, and you have performed above and beyond what anyone could have expected. But I'm going to ask more."

All around the crowd, people stood a little taller, jaws set and brows furrowed. Daws had called them to action and they were going to come through, no matter what. At this juncture, the thought of disappointing Daws was worse than any threat of punishment he could have come up with.

"We still have one of these vermin loose on our soil. While we've been disposing of this creature," he gestured again to Shawen, "Shriver, the fire Tannik has been rampaging through our country. Night is falling, I'm sure you crave the comforts of home, but this is war. Get what rest you can, but we are going to be hunting Shriver and battering him into submission, just as we did with this one."

He gave Shawen's body one more nudge with his foot, then he stepped over her to stand in front of the crowd.

"Anyone who doubts our victory can leave now."

No one person budged. None even looked side to side at the others. Every man and woman in the crowd stared steadily back at Daws, pledging their allegiance with their firmly fixed feet.

"Then let me make my intentions perfectly clear. I will kill Shriver. I will stand over his dead body and smile. But I would not count it victory if I stopped there. I hereby declare war on the Tanniks!"

More cheering…

"Any that dare invade our homeland will be destroyed!"
Louder cheering…

168

"But I will bring the war to them in their own land! I will hunt them like the animals they are. They have ruled by fear for centuries. They will learn to fear us before we grind their vile race out of existence!"

This is how a holy war starts, I thought to myself. A noble hero, a perfect villain, and a righteous cause. It also came as a shock for me. I had only been thinking about whether or not Daws would be able to defeat Shriver.

If what he said was true, he had already moved past that point in his mind and was now plotting a counter-invasion. Somehow, in spite of all my predictions and evaluations, I had still managed to underestimate Daws's ambitions.

For all his talk, after Daws had finished his speech, his next move was not a glorious march against Shriver, but a hasty cleanup of the park. He used one of the abandoned buildings as a temporary shelter so the soldiers could sleep.

Daws secured a room far from the others and our original council convened. Even Kip was invited in again, though he shot Yrris a dirty look as he settled into a chair in the corner, holding a sturdy ceramic cooking pot that was Chuck's new home.

"A little the worse for wear," Daws observed drily as he looked around the room. Bandages and tattered clothes were now the common theme. "Except for you, Phillip, you look about the same."

I shrugged. "Just lucky, I guess."

"Well, if you figure out how to share with the rest of us, please do so. You don't even look tired."

"You got it, boss."

Our light-hearted exchange finished up the small talk and Daws got right back to business.

"Lori, you mentioned you had a question, possibly an idea. Would you like to share with us?"

"Yes, sir," Lori responded. She had managed to find a clean uniform and wash her face, but the smell of storm drain still clung to her and a few flecks of mud spotted her blonde hair.

"Tratch, I managed to see a bit of the main explosion from afar and it looked like there were tiny flashes of light in the blast. Was that your doing? One of your chemicals?"

"In a way, yes, but not directly," Tratch explained. "We had to put everything together quickly, but I found some tools the workers had been using during the construction. I put them on top of my charges. It was all I could think of for shrapnel."

"I'm not quite following," Daws interjected. "How would tools create flashes of light?"

"The measuring equipment," Tratch answered. "Many of the tools that have to bend around corners use magnesium ribbon for reinforcement."

"And magnesium is a flammable metal," Lori finished the explanation. "It burns several times hotter than fire, even several times hotter than most of our incendiary launchers."

"I see," Daws smiled. "So we might have our method of burning Shriver, eh? Where can we get a large supply of magnesium?"

Tratch rolled out his maps on the table and searched them while the rest of us watched on in silence. I had tried to translate for Yrris, but she wasn't familiar with magnesium. She had pointed to the small iron buttons on her own clothes and I shook my head. She accepted the fact that they had something that could burn hot enough to hurt Shriver and that was all she cared to know for the time being.

"There!" Tratch thrust his finger at a point on the map. "It's a medical equipment factory. Many of the blades they use for surgery are made of magnesium, though I couldn't tell you why. The ceramic models are sharper."

Lori couldn't resist inserting a quick explanation.

"It's an issue of flexibility. When ceramic gets very thin, as some of those scalpels need to be, it gets brittle and there's risk of chipping. Even if it hits a bone and bends a little, a magnesium blade would still remain whole, not dropping anything into the patient."

"And there you go," Tratch quipped. "The point is, that factory would have literally tons of magnesium on hand. A branch of the lab was working on a fire suppression system for it, should the magnesium ever catch fire. They were having a devil of a time of it, too. Almost nothing stops magnesium once it gets going."

"Then that's our weapon," Daws said decisively. "Everyone get a couple hours of sleep. I need you sharp. I hate leaving Shriver to rampage, but if we don't get this right the first time, we may not get a second chance. We've been lucky so far, but we can't depend on that."

The group needed no urging. Kip didn't even move from his spot, he only laid down, curling up around Chuck. In less than a minute, his soft snoring filled the room. Everyone else scattered to wherever they could find a free corner or an abandoned bed. I found a nice foldable cot, laid down, and waited for two hours to pass.

We only got one hour.

Chapter 23

In war, misdirection can cause as much damage as bullets.
                    –Musings of the Historian

The sound of small arms fire and shouted alarms sprang everyone from their beds while darkness still claimed the area. Tratch took immediate command, organizing soldiers and barking orders.

I caught his arm as he ran by.

"What's going on?" I asked him. He shook my hand loose irritably and snapped at me as he continued past.

"The old government still has a few commanders trying to take us down." Then he was gone.

I had forgotten entirely about the civil war Daws had instigated when he ordered the execution of the Oligarchs. We had seen General Hines die, but it stood to reason that there would still be other factions loyal to the prior government who would still be hunting Daws as a traitor.

I heard Daws's growls of frustration before I saw him round the corner, doing up the last few buttons on his uniform.

"Ungrateful swine…" I heard him mutter under his breath as he too flew by on his way to oversee the night battle.

I wandered the empty rooms, searching for a familiar face. I smiled when I found Kip, right where we had left him, sleeping peacefully. He had one arm circling Chuck, who seemed to be recovering well in his new pot.

172

I let him sleep. Witnessing his first battlefield flashback had been heartbreaking enough. I had no desire to trigger a second episode.

I wandered from room to room, but only ran into soldiers running one way or another. Daws's full army was still a fair distance away. We had only brought a few select squadrons on this mission. The bulk were with the rest of Yrris' people at the main headquarters. So we were likely outnumbered.

This line of thought also reminded me of something else I wasn't seeing. While I saw soldiers coming and going, and plenty of empty rooms, I didn't see Yrris or a single one of her people.

Finally giving up on seeing the battle through the eyes of one of the others, I decided to find a good spot and watch it unfold on my own.

The great thing about active battles is that they're usually pretty easy to find. I followed the noises and running soldiers until I found a window facing the right direction. I kept the lights in the room off, so as not to draw attention to myself. It would distract from the story if I had enemy soldiers trying to kill me.

Even outnumbered, our side had the advantage. The building we were in provided us with ample cover from gunfire. It also gave us the high ground, and sharpshooters near the top were picking off enemy soldiers down below, who could find little cover in the empty park.

The battle was already settling into a sort of lull as initial positions were fortified and supplies were seen to. No doubt their intention had been to catch us sleeping. They had underestimated Tratch. Even exhausted and flush with victory, he had still taken the time to set up a rotating watch and a roving patrol.

Suddenly Lori was at my elbow.

"I should have known I'd find you here," she whispered.

"Where?" I asked, glancing around the room, trying to discern its importance.

"At the best possible location to observe the battle. It took me a while to sort it out, but you do it naturally, don't you?"

I shrugged. "I enjoy a good vantage point as much as the next crazy person."

Even in the dark, I could see her roll her eyes.

"You're not crazy. Don't think you've fooled anyone. I've got a team of my best people working on figuring out who you are, Phillip. They've never failed me before."

I smiled broadly, genuinely amused at the idea.

"They sound wonderful. I'd love to meet them in person sometime."

"Why?" she asked, confused at my jovial response to being told I was a subject of a full government investigation.

"Mostly to apologize," I answered. "It must be a sad thing for such an elite team to have their perfect record marred."

"You think you're so clever," she scolded. "Either you think you've covered your tracks too well to be discovered, or you're this confident because you're not from this world. Don't look so surprised. With the Vortex opening up, we're analyzing all sorts of new options. I've even got one person dedicated specifically to analyzing the possibilities of you being this 'First' that has Yrris so scared."

"I'm not the First," I assured her. She nodded cautiously.

"Both the research and my own instincts tend to agree with you. The profile doesn't quite fit. However, you should know that one popular theory is that you are a minor Tannik, using us to eliminate rivals."

"That would be very clever of me," I admitted. "The Tannik hierarchy seems very set. If I wanted to move up in the ranks, I'd have to figure out some kind of outside help."

She nodded and I continued.

"Though you would still have a problem with the timeline. By now you've got abundant witnesses that say I started living in that apartment months before the Vortex formed."

"It's your best defense," she admitted. "But it's still not air-tight, since we're still trying to figure out how the Vortex opened in the first place."

I perked up at this.

"What have you discovered so far?"

Her eyes narrowed, suspicious of my sudden interest.

"Very little," she confessed. "We've been scrambling on that point. The research team that would have had the best chance of explaining all of this went missing."

"Missing?" I said, incredulous. "When did they go missing? And how does a high end group of physicists go missing?"

"It's a smaller group than you'd think, and funded through some fairly secret channels. It's not the first time they've suddenly been gone for a month or two. Then they return and everyone acts like it was perfectly normal. It's not that uncommon with government work."

"Maybe so," I commented. "But it seems awfully convenient for the Tanniks."

"Perhaps," she agreed, but offered no more information or insight. Already, her attention was elsewhere, her stare out the window becoming more focused. While she hadn't been slouching, she was suddenly standing straighter, ever fiber of her body tensing.

She swore bitterly and ran from the room. After a moment or two of searching, I saw what her sharp eyes had seen first: launchers.

They were far back, tucked amongst the buildings on the other side of the park. I had assumed that the lackluster battle happening in the square was because they had lost the element of surprise, but now I saw the battle for what is was--a distraction. The front line wasn't holding back because they lacked ambition, they were only there to draw fire and attention away from the launcher teams that were setting up back in the darkness.

From past experience, I knew that launcher teams do not set up or move very quickly. Their mortars were clumsy, early prototypes, nothing to compare to the nimble mobile artillery I had seen on more advanced worlds.

Still, though ponderous, they were effective. They would rain explosives and napalm down on us from a safe distance until the building itself crumpled and buried us all. And that would be the best case scenario. If they were feeling desperate, they would bombard us with chemicals and pathogens and all here would die choking.

A sudden increase of weapons fire told me that either Lori had found Tratch and Daws to report the launchers, or they had seen them on their own. There was an intensity to the battle now. Our own troops now fought to split the enemy line so they could break through and attack the launchers before they finished setting up.

Sadly, there wasn't much to hope for in that regard. Our troops had been holding their own easily enough in the battle, but that was entirely due to the cover they enjoyed firing from inside the building. Outside, they would be outnumbered and outgunned.

I was watching one of the launchers. It was difficult to make out details in the dark, but it looked nearly completed. A soldier was loading the canisters of gas that they used as a propellant. The next step was to aim and fire.

But then, inexplicably, the launcher tipped over onto its side. Men scrambled around it, either trying to stop it or to get out of its way. There was no violent explosion, no thundering crash, it was even a fairly slow process. The launcher suddenly laid on its side. We had been granted a few more minutes.

Between two other buildings, another launcher was almost finished. This one, too, tipped over slowly as they were loading the propellant canisters. It was bizarre, it was unexplainable...

...it was magic.

Suddenly I knew where Yrris and her people had gone. They didn't have guns or military training, but they had their magic. It was meager and useless against the might of the Tanniks. But attacking from the darkness of the alleys, it was wonderfully effective against the launchers.

Now that I knew what to look for, I could see the outline of the mounds of dirt that had suddenly risen up underneath each of the tipped launchers. I had only witnessed Yrris' air elemental power, but it stood to reason that others of her people would have some basic power over earth or stone.

The launcher crews were much more panicked now. Some joined other teams, trying to get a launcher completed faster. Others dug at the mounds, suspecting some sort of trickery or hidden tunnels full of soldiers. None of them thought to search the nearby alleys and shadows.

Above me and to the left, a chant started among Daws's

soldiers.

"HAHK TAH JAY RAH! HAHK TAH JAY RAH!..." The sounds were ominous and dark, especially as more voices took up the chant. It was clearly a foreign tongue, though it confused me that there could be a language that I would not understand. Then it hit me...

It was gibberish.

Chapter 24

In politics, perception is much more important than are facts.
–Musings of the Historian

Daws must have seen the launchers being tipped over, just as I had. Eventually, the launcher teams, finding no other reason for the moving ground, would start looking around and would find the real culprits.

Rather than wait for that to happen, Daws was supplying the opposing soldiers with a reason for the strange happenings. He was giving them a sham magic. Everyone in the nation would have heard by now about the otherworldly forces at work. They would have heard about the dark cloud that ripped people to shreds. They would have heard about the fiery mountain that devoured entire buildings with its inferno.

Their minds would already be prepared to accept the idea of magic, so now Daws was giving it to them. Once the chanting had passed through to all of the soldiers, it could be heard across the park. I saw a couple of the soldiers who had been digging into the dirt mounds cautiously back away.

A sudden gust of wind washed over the soldiers below. It wasn't strong enough to knock them over. It wasn't even strong enough to spoil their aim; but it was sudden and unnatural in the still night. A minute later, another gust blew over the soldiers, but going the opposite direction.

Uncertainty would start to creep into their minds now. The

launcher teams would be first, as they had seen the most direct effect of the magic. The other soldiers wouldn't be too far behind, though. As the battle wore on, they would start to wonder why the launcher teams were taking so long. Then they would glance back and see the tipped equipment, or possibly even see the teams already gone, having run away.

Then the panic would start to seep in, and that was the true end of any battle. History was packed with stories of smaller forces turning away larger armies. In the end, it wasn't about the numbers of soldiers on the field, it was the confidence and determination of the soldiers to continue fighting until the victory was won. The army that lost heart always lost the battle shortly after, regardless of all other advantages of numbers, position, or strategy.

Daws couldn't do much to chip away at their numbers, so he was chipping away at their courage. They would need something dramatic though, to instigate a full retreat. Otherwise, this battle could turn into a siege, which we wouldn't be prepared to withstand. This was only a pit stop before we rejoined the main force.

Then Lady Yrris took a great risk. I moved closer to the window as I saw her and another man I didn't recognize crawling across the ground near the park. It was nerve-wracking to watch. I realized that they wouldn't be as obvious to the soldiers on the ground, who were digging in to whatever scant cover they could find, but from my lofty viewpoint, it looked like they could simply glance over and see her at any time.

I took comfort in the fact that they were scooting along, bellies on the ground, and they had the massive crater from the attack on Shawen between them and the main line of attacking soldiers.

They had nearly made the rim of the blast crater and I worried that somehow they hadn't understood the dangers of the chemicals inside. I breathed a sigh of relief when they stopped just short of the edge.

The man reached his hands out and laid still. I watched for a very slow two minutes as very little seemed to be happening. Then, a small pillar rose out of the crater, a small concavity at the top glinted in the dim light and I pictured the thick, slimy chemicals pooled at the top of the column.

Yrris then raised her hands and I realized her intentions. Even if the plan worked, she ran a great risk of being discovered and shot. I wondered why she had chosen herself for such a perilous mission. Then I realized that the risk was exactly why she had taken it for herself. She wouldn't ask any of her people to do such a foolhardy thing.

A concentrated blast of air hit the top of the raised column of dirt, blowing specks over the line of soldiers like sand blown from the hand of a child.

Screams rippled through the lines of soldiers as the dirt settled over them. It likely wouldn't be fatal, or even cause great injury. The amount of chemical coating a single speck of dirt would burn tiny holes in the skin, but probably not much more. Tratch hadn't included any biological pathogens. In the worst case, a few molecules worth would enter the bloodstream and the soldier would feel like his blood was boiling inside of him.

If the soldiers had a chance to recover from the pain and realize the direction of the attack, Yrris and her friend would be in great danger. Fortunately, Daws was ready.

An explosion ripped up from the ground about fifty yards

181

from the line of soldiers. I recognized it as the Delta position from our earlier explosive traps. It was in the wrong position to do any real damage, but the psychological effect it had as it rained dust and debris down on the soldiers was catastrophic. With pinpoints of burning pain already searing into their flesh, they no doubt imagined that the blast and the falling dirt would mean even more torment.

They broke and ran wildly. Most didn't even bother to run back toward the cover of the buildings. This wasn't a retreat, it was a stampede. They scrambled and trampled over one another in a mad dash to get clear of the area. Daws's sharpshooters took advantage of the chaos and more of the projectile pellets shot through the terrified mass below.

The shooters were aiming low now, looking to wound, not to kill. Ten minutes ago, a pellet through the leg would have been treated as an expected battlefield wound and treated as such. Now, in this new terrifying world of magic, each wound was received with panicked screaming as the soldiers imagined new horrors stalking them in the darkness.

Just like that, the opposing army was broken, fleeing into the night to spread stories of Daws's terrible new power. Whatever was left of the opposition wasn't likely to last for long. Daws could have massacred the entire army in that park with conventional weapons and it wouldn't have had such a profound effect as what had happened.

Kip laughed uproariously as I told him the details of the night's battle and he told me about the jokes Chuck was making about mosquitoes chasing off elephants. Daws and Tratch were in similar good humor. It had been a tremendous victory.

Even better, we were at full strength again. Yrris had seen

that the battle might go long and she had sent runners to get the rest of the army. Due to the language barrier, her messengers hadn't been able to explain what was going on, but they had been able to say, "Daws!" over and over again while pointing in the direction of the park.

It had been enough. The army had made a forced march in the middle of the night to get to our location. They were tired and a little grouchy to have missed the battle, but they were ready to go.

The rest of Yrris' people had come as well and our group moved out toward the factory as a mighty force. As we marched, I took the opportunity to wander through the ranks. Stories about the battle with Shawen were passing from soldier to soldier like wildfire, as well as reports about the night battle. The respect that the soldiers had felt for Daws before was quickly turning into something like sacred reverence.

We reached the factory without any further incidents and teams of soldiers spread out through the factory to ferret out where the stores of magnesium were kept.

Meanwhile, Daws, Tratch, and Lori remained outside to discuss their next move.

"How are we going to weaponize the magnesium once we've got it?" Daws was asking Lori as I walked up. I had become such a customary member of the team that none of them even missed a beat in their conversation as I sidled in.

"If we can get our hands on a couple launchers," Tratch started, "we could probably retrofit them to launch the magnesium in acid tubes. We'd drain the acid first, of course."

"There are two problems with that," Lori argued. "First of all, we don't have any launchers here right now, and our closest launchers are in the opposite direction of where we need to go to intercept Shriver. Those teams don't exactly move fast.

"Secondly, heat rises," she continued. "If we're trying to get his temperature high enough to destroy whatever serves to hold his intelligence, raining magnesium down on top of him from above might not be enough. Most of the energy released by the combustion would be wasted, traveling up and away from our target."

"So we go from below." Tratch shifted plans effortlessly. He didn't let his pride get in the way of finding the best way to attack his enemies. "Do we have any way of luring him towards us, like we did with Shawen?"

"I don't think it'd be the same," Daws chimed in. "Shawen was a cruel, sadistic being. When she attacked, she moved in close. She wanted to see the pain she caused. When Shriver attacked, however, he was going for intimidation, a big show.

"Remember when he attacked, he shot out his flame arms to engulf our launcher teams. His center didn't shift at all. That's not the sort of enemy that is going to follow bait. He'll counterattack if he sees a threat, but he's not here for the people; that was going to be Shawen's job. He's here to wreak havoc on the buildings and infrastructure. He doesn't need to run around after people to do that."

"Then it's even easier," Tratch concluded. "We only need to get ahead of him and plant the magnesium where we know he's going to be. I'm not even sure we need to be as careful hiding this trap, he doesn't seem to be as intelligent as Shawen. More brute force, trusting to his power."

Shouts came from the factory. They had found the magnesium, cases and cases of it. It was stored in little ingots to be

184

melted down later very carefully under special fluxes that would keep oxygen clear of the process, lest the magnesium catch fire.

"I think we've got a plan, then," Daws said and the party started to break up. He caught at Tratch's arm and pulled him back. "Do we still have active communication with our other teams?"

"It's starting to get a little patchy, sir. With all of the evacuations, nobody is seeing to the upkeep of the polymer network. With all the buildings Shriver has destroyed, it's getting a little thin in some areas, which means the signal has to travel farther for the workarounds."

"Do we still have the vital connections?" Daws asked, his voice suddenly lower. Tratch nodded and his voice returned to normal.

"Can you get in touch with the engineers?" Daws asked.

"I can certainly try, but they're going to be too far away to help us place magnesium for Shriver. We'll have to do the best we can with what we've got."

"That isn't what I had in mind," Daws corrected him. "I'd like a building around the Vortex again, even a temporary one."

"That should be simple enough, sir. We left most of the building supplies behind when Shawen came through. But is that really a priority right now?"

Daws only nodded for a response and Tratch started talking to his men, getting his communicator and its connection lines tied in to the local polymer network. It was a rugged piece of equipment and Tratch had hauled the thing all over the city on our many adventures, keeping Daws tied in at a national level. The extensive polymer network was a true wonder of infrastructure. Seldom had I seen any common utility so overbuilt.

It seemed like every street and building had crisscrossing lines of the stuff running every which way.

The magnesium was loaded onto carts and our army took off again, this time with even more purpose. We were marching to battle. The mood was electric--the men believed they couldn't lose with Daws at the lead.

Chapter 25

Most of life's greatest rewards belong, not to the strong or intelligent, but to the patient and persistent.
      –Musings of the Historian

Even without the reports Tratch had gathered from his lookouts across the city, it would have been childishly easy to figure out where Shriver had gone. Apparently lacking in imagination, he had continued in a straight line, destroying buildings as he went.

He clearly enjoyed his work and had taken plenty of time at each building, making sure each was reduced to smoking rubble before he moved on. Many people think that concrete buildings would be immune to fire like that, but they are wrong. The chemical bonds that hold concrete together break down under intense heat and it crumbles under its own weight.

These buildings were even more susceptible to destruction by fire than other concrete buildings I had seen on other worlds. On planets with more metal, the concrete was usually reinforced by metal bars, usually iron or steel that helped compensate for concrete's inherently brittle nature.

On this world, they laced their concrete with networks of woven carbon-based fibers. These fiber networks looked filmy and frail, but actually surpassed steel in tensile strength. The result was incredibly durable concrete that could be stacked as high as needed, though the carbon fiber broke down under heat much faster than steel would have.

We knew how far we were from Shriver by the temperature of the smoldering piles. As we passed piles that were still smoking, we branched off from the main trail and took a much wider path around to avoid detection.

Even with buildings blocking our view and considerable distance between us, we could still see occasional gouts of flame rise above the buildings as Shriver continued his destructive spree through the city.

Undoubtedly, he had never seen anything like this city. It was likely that he was heading outward in a straight line to get an idea of how large the city was, like a child running through a playground first to see his options.

We got ahead of him and the soldiers broke open the crates of magnesium. They spread the ingots out in a wide swath where Shriver would be passing, holding back about a third of the crates for backup, should they need to come up with other options in a hurry.

We didn't have long to wait for the big reveal. We heard Shriver coming before we saw him, the roaring flames sounding like an approaching forest fire. The army had retreated back amongst the other buildings, peeking out around corners to watch the result of our preparations.

The soldiers were visibly disappointed as Shriver moved over the shining ingots with no effect. They were used to traps and mines that blew up on contact, or spewed acid and poisons. Compared to such spectacle, the ingots of magnesium were quite anticlimactic.

They didn't have the benefit of Lori's science lecture, which had explained in abundant detail the natural delay that would happen as the magnesium dispersed the heat through itself and partially into the ground below. It wouldn't start reacting until the entire brick had heated up enough to allow one corner to reach its combustion temperature.

This would actually work to our advantage, she had explained. Shriver would be well-positioned over the ingots by the time they ignited. All of the heat would transfer directly upward into the center of the mass of heat and smoke.

Sure enough, Shriver had already traveled nearly ten yards past the first ingot before we saw the first point of light. Shriver himself was already bright enough that everyone was squinting to look at him, but that ingot of magnesium lit up with an entirely new level of light and heat.

From the depth of Shriver's roiling flames, we saw a spot of pure white light. Shriver's own flame suddenly seemed dark by comparison. Then others started to ignite and soon the whole base of Shriver was shining with brilliant stars of light, like pure angels trying to escape a dark purgatory.

Once again, the soldiers were disappointed if they were expecting an immediate reaction. Shriver didn't seem to notice the extra heat. He actually seemed to grow larger, as if feeding off of the donated fuel. Some of the faces around me started to turn somber. Perhaps we had made a serious mistake.

Then Shriver grew even bigger, his clumsy arms thrashing furiously.

"He's trying to disperse some of the excess heat," Lori guessed. "He probably hasn't noticed the source yet."

It was hard to tell at first, due to the massive size of the flames, but then Tratch noticed a change.

"He's moving backward," he said softly, then louder. "He's

moving backward! He's seen the magnesium. We need more magnesium behind him, now, now, NOW!"

Tratch was yelling and pushing nearby soldiers towards the remaining crates. They caught his urgency and the crates were shoved from the carts, breaking on the ground and spilling magnesium ingots all over like a silvery flood. They gathered handfuls of the light metal and rushed forward, heedless of their own safety.

They threw ingots as fast as they could grab them. Other soldiers saw what was going on and jumped in to help. In their haste, they got too close and Shriver saw them. A fiery arm lashed out and an entire rank of hurling soldiers were wiped away by cleansing flames.

The soldiers behind them roared their defiance, fully carried away in the adrenaline of battle. They continued throwing the ingots.

"He's coming this way!" Tratch roared. "Fall back! Keep throwing the magnesium!"

The soldiers complied instantly, as if the orders had been their own thoughts. The remaining carts were pulled back and the crates of magnesium ingots were dispersed amongst the soldiers with remarkable swiftness.

Training was showing now as they adjusted to this new form of warfare. These men knew what it was to face down enemy fire, to remain calm even as explosions erupted all around and friends died on either side.

Even though no one was calling the cadence, the throwing now took on the distinct feel of volleys as soldiers lined up and threw together. Once they had thrown, they stepped back, in between another rank of soldiers, who were ready with their own volley. The orderly retreat left a glittering path of magnesium in front of Shriver.

Bright points of light shone underneath him now and the extra heat continued to show. He was larger than we had ever seen him, a thrashing inferno trying to transfer some of the energy beneath into the atmosphere above. Thick smoke choked the air above us and blotted out the sun, casting us all in shadow. Another wild lunge took out another squad of soldiers, but the line did not break, and the motion carried Shriver over even more ingots of our incinerating metal.

The thrashing increased and Shriver stopped advancing.

"He's hurt and confused," Daws shouted over the roaring flames. "Those who dare, get more magnesium under him!"

It wasn't an order, it was a call for heroes, a reckless charge against certain death. Nearly a hundred soldiers broke ranks, grabbing extra ingots from those around them.

One of them, a nameless patriot, raised an ingot over his head in a defiant salute.

"For Daws! And the death of the Tanniks!" he shouted, his voice surprisingly young. The other volunteers took up the battle cry and they rushed together into close enough range to throw the light ingots directly into the flames of Shriver.

I don't know if the counter-strike I witnessed next was intentional or merely a random lashing of a demon in pain, but a lance of fire raked over the soldiers and most fell to the ground, burned or overcome with the inhalation of heat and smoke.

Only a dozen or so were able to stagger back to the lines. Shriver did not follow. He didn't even move to get away from the dozens of new white-hot furnaces burning below him.

The flames, which had been bold and yellow before, were

smaller now, red and full of black smoke.

"He's getting smaller!" Daws shouted the observation to Lori, following up with a question. "Is it working? Is he dying?"

Lori took only the time of a single breath to study the shrinking inferno before she came up with an answer.

"I don't think that's it, sir," she shouted back. "Look, even the ingots aren't glowing as brightly. He's running out of oxygen. I have no idea how he had enough to do this in the first place, but the extra heat and the magnesium are taxing him. Even the extra smoke is choking him out!"

"So what do we do? More magnesium?"

Another moment's pause.

"I think we already have enough. Sir, I think the flames are getting small enough that they aren't providing the protection they used to. We might be able to penetrate to the core now."

"Right! Tratch, see to it," Daws ordered. Tratch turned to the ranks of soldiers.

"DRAW!" The yell was so loud and raw that Tratch must have felt the strain of it all the way to the bottom of his lungs. Hundreds of soldiers ripped their sidearms from their waists like starving men grasping at crusts.

"STAGGERED VOLLEYS ONE BY FIVE! FIRST AT EYE ZERO! RISING BY TWOS, SEARCHING FIRE! COMMENCE!"

What followed was military exactness, trained to perfection. The first rank fired a volley just as Tratch yelled "commence." The second rank fired in perfect unison, one second behind the first and aiming a tiny bit higher. The third rank hit their volley perfectly one second after that, again lifting their target slightly more than the previous line.

The pattern continued through the fifth rank of soldiers, at which point the first rank started again. The firing was so steady and unified that it sounded more like a single man doing a slow clap than hundreds of soldiers firing weapons.

On the trip over, I had learned more about the new weapons. Apparently, the fiber pellets they used as ammunition were somewhat unstable, tending to break apart mid-flight.

This was problem for long-range accuracy, so sharpshooters used special ceramic bullets. However, for short range battles and large volleys, it only meant more projectiles in the air.

On the second round, when the third line of soldiers loosed their volley, there was a distinctive twitch from Shriver.

"NOTE TARGET! REFOCUS AND BARRAGE! COMMENCE!"

The barrage command must have implied a free-for-all, because every soldier there, including Tratch, aimed his weapon at the new target area and pulled the trigger repeatedly as fast as it would respond. I could already see some of the faster soldiers reloading cartridges into their weapons, having already expended all of the pellets in their furious attack.

I suspected that an incredibly small percentage of the fired projectiles actually made contact, but they were starting to have an effect. The flames had lost all form now, no arms or head. The bulk of Shriver's mass was no longer flame, but thick black smoke as he choked for oxygen. The remaining flames jumped and jerked as the controlling entity, hidden somewhere in the middle of the inferno, was wounded and distracted.

Shriver had been so mighty and terrible that it felt like his ending should be something dramatic and shocking, like a sudden explosion or last-ditch effort that nearly let him escape.

Instead it was a surprisingly gradual affair. The

magnesium ingots burned out, but the vast fires did not reignite. The power behind them was hurt, possibly even dead already, but there was a momentum to the flames and the fires continued to burn and throb around the center.

The soldiers continued to fire their barrage, reloading cartridges of pellets when they ran out, but there was no slowing or redirection of force. Their current course of action was having the desired effect, so they didn't deviate from it. They settled into their task like lumberjacks chopping down a mighty tree, each emptied cartridge of pellets was like another stroke of the axe.

The end was so gradual that everyone started to look a little bored with it, which was ridiculous, considering the magnitude of what they were doing. By the time the flames finally died down, the soldiers had already started working in shifts, giving certain ranks a rest and an opportunity to see to their ammunition supply.

Finally the last of the flames were gone, but there was no clear ending to prompt a cheer. Tratch raised a fist to stop the barrage and he ordered everyone at ease. Once more, it was our original party that approached the fallen Shriver through the last wisps of smoke.

The first impression I had was that of a large lump of obsidian, black and shiny. Shriver was shaped like a man in the broadest sense, but that's where the similarities stopped. The outer surface was hard as rock and lacked defining features. There was a head and a flat place where a face would be, but there were no features, no mouth or eyes to suggest any common roots with humanity.

Chapter 26

From the outside, it's awfully hard to tell the difference between bravery and stupidity.

-Musings of the Historian

"How could such a thing even be alive?" Daws asked.

"I think he was molten," Lori suggested. "At the height of his power, he was probably as mobile as anyone. It's an oversimplification, but imagine his blood being like lava. When he cooled, he hardened."

"How did we even kill it?" Tratch wondered. "I don't see any markings on the surface. Not a drop of blood anywhere. I don't think my weapon could even dent that surface."

Before waiting for an answer, he tried it, drawing his sidearm and firing a round off Shriver's chest. As Tratch had predicted, the pellet burst into tiny pieces on the hard black surface without leaving a mark. Lori took a moment inspecting the body before she offered her analysis.

"This might sound a little odd, but I think we poisoned him."

"How's that?" Daws asked.

"I think the pellets could penetrate a little when he was still in his molten state, but they would have been broken down in the heat. Still, the materials would have gotten into his bloodstream. Look at these cloudy lines running under the surface. I think those might be his veins, or whatever his equivalent of veins were."

"So you're saying that our barrage that lasted for almost a

full hour only managed to murk up this guy's blood a little?"
Tratch sounded unconvinced, but Lori didn't catch it. She barreled on, excited as the possibilities unfolded in her mind.

"Yes, exactly! It makes more sense as I think about it. Even though it was happening at much higher temperatures than we're used to, this was still life. He probably had organs that performed different functions in his body, just like ours.

"The amount of protections his body must have had to withstand all that heat would have made him impervious to most regular forms of physical harm, but his body still had to function--life is always complex. If we managed to inject the foreign material of our pellets, it would corrupt all of the balances and chemical reactions that kept him running. If you think about it, a mere air bubble injected into our veins is enough to stop our hearts. We did a lot more than an air bubble here."

"What about his face?" Daws interjected. "Any theories on why he wouldn't have eyes or ears?"

"I've got a theory, but without testing, I can't be sure. I suspect that there was a face, but it was molten, or at least very soft. If it was one of the last things to harden and he was lying on his back, dying, his features would have settled flat, like a bowl of pudding."

"His face sunk into itself?" Tratch asked incredulously. "That's downright unsettling. Shouldn't we at least see his eyes?"

"Not necessarily." Lori continued. "Regular eyes like we think about them wouldn't have been able to see through all that fire and smoke anyway. It's much more likely that he had something closer to sensors, maybe operating on higher wavelengths, like ultraviolet, that would be able to penetrate all the flames.

196

"It could also explain why he seemed less intelligent. It's possible that he was as intelligent as any of them, but his senses were rudimentary. He might have only been seeing vague shapes."

"Traded his sight for power, eh?" Daws commented. "Are we thinking he was like Shawen, human at some point?"

"I'd say so," Lori agreed. "You can see that he had to change his physical makeup to adapt to life at high heat, but he still tried to maintain his human form. There's no strategic advantage to that shape, so I'm guessing he was trying to look normal in his own eyes."

"If he was looking to look normal, he failed," Tratch observed drily. "He looks like the kind of art piece fancy people try to impress their friends with."

I smiled at his colorful comparison. Hearing it, all I could see was a fairly impressive abstract statue lying on the ground.

"Well that's that," said Daws with a tone of finality. "Let's tell everyone that Shriver is dead."

The speech Daws gave to the troops about Shriver's death was also fairly stirring, but it lacked the energy of the one he gave over the body of Shawen. That had been a battle against a vicious demon, a contest for the fate of both worlds. Emotions had been particularly powerful.

This time, everyone's confidence had been absurdly high. Everyone here believed in their ultimate victory. Daws had fulfilled his image of an unstoppable force. So the battle to kill Shriver hadn't truly felt like a battle at all. It had been closer to a hunt, stalking and bringing down some dangerous beast. Even the heroic casualties had been taken in stride.

These weren't soldiers and refugees now, they were crusaders. They were part of something bigger. Sacrifices would naturally be a part of that life and none of them were backing down from the cost.

Daws's soldiers and the Argothians now stood ready and awaiting their next orders. Our little war council stood, listened, and, in my case, translated as Daws laid out his next steps.

"Lori, who do we have that can write? I need this whole story put into something we can circulate. All the regular print and distribution channels have been shut down or evacuated, so the people have no real clue of what's going on. Let's use our own resources, get something printed up, and use the soldiers to circulate. Tratch, how many soldiers would you need to do a fair blanket of the city?"

"We've got some support personnel who would be a bit more fitted to that kind of task, but even if we use all of them, I'm going to have to take some of this force if we want it to get it out quickly," Tratch responded. Daws was already nodding as he replied.

"We want it out quickly; assign who you need. I'll miss the combat troops, but it would actually be a good thing if some of these soldiers were out among the public, giving their own accounts."

"Yes, sir," Tratch responded and started to turn away, but Daws stopped him.

"Hold on, you'll have more orders than that to give. I'm also going to need your most elite forces with you and me. We're going back through the Vortex."

"Back, sir?" Lori interrupted. "With troops? I know you told the people you were planning on making war against the Tanniks, but is this really the best time? We're stretched thin already, we've lost a lot of support, and the transition isn't complete. Getting the story out will have a lot of people thinking you're a hero, but they might not be as quick to hand you the country."

"Trust me, Lori. Now is the perfect time. We have to strike while the momentum is in our favor. If the Tanniks realize their champions are down, it might be enough to bring out this First everyone is so afraid of. If we take him down, I believe the rest will fall easily."

"That's your plan?" Lori was incredulous. "After we barely managed to defeat these two, your plan is to go after their boss? Yrris is no coward, and I've seen her face when she talks about the First. She's scared, more scared than I've ever seen her.

"I know there have been some dramatic victories here, but the fact is that we've been incredibly lucky. We can't depend on that. Do you really want to risk everything you've achieved so far to challenge a being like the First?"

"Don't count us out just yet," Daws smiled, like it was all a big joke. "These Tanniks are awe-inspiring, it's true, and we have enjoyed a great deal of luck so far; but I'd also like to point out that when the power died away, they were still only people. They got so powerful that they started to take it for granted. They haven't learned to work together like we have. I think when we see the First, he'll be even bigger and scarier than these, but he'll still be mortal, and he'll still fall, like these have."

"How can you be so confident?" Lori was getting a little heated. "Tratch, help me out here! Would you walk into a fight without knowing your enemy? We should be sealing up the Vortex in concrete, maybe even banding the concrete in iron--if we can afford such a thing--until we can deal with some of the things here."

"Actually," Tratch drawled. "I'm with Daws on this one.

Let's smoke this First guy out and finish the job. If he's dead, I'm not sure the others will even try fighting us."

Lori looked from one man to the other, trying to understand why her two friends, who had always seemed so reasonable, were now throwing caution to the wind in a reckless bid for glory.

Her eyes shifted to me, then Kip. I could almost see her thoughts play across her eyes as if typed there in bold print. She was evaluating the likelihood of convincing us to join her side. Finally, she dismissed us entirely. Even if she succeeded, we wouldn't have any impact pulling Daws from his intended course. Why Daws even kept the two of us in his inner council was still something of a mystery.

Finally, she turned to Yrris, though she addressed me.

"Phillip, would you please tell Lady Yrris what Daws and Tratch are proposing?"

"Why not?" I responded, turning to Yrris, who was already deeply concerned at witnessing the heated discussion. "Lady Yrris, Daws and Tratch want to pick a fight with the First. They think that if they beat him, the other Tanniks will fall."

Yrris went immediately pale.

"Phillip, tell them not to do this. Our only real hope of survival in all this was to escape through the Vortex to this world and somehow seal it behind us. Daws can certainly handle most of the remaining Tanniks, but if he's thinking he can handle the First like the others, he's wrong and he'll die!"

"She says that if you try to face the First, you'll die. She seems pretty darn certain about it," I reported to Daws. He was not moved.

"Tell her to believe in me a little while longer. While you're at it, tell Lori, too. Maybe she'll listen to you."

200

Lori actually growled in her frustration.

"Fine," she bit off the word and spoke through clenched teeth. "If you want to die, I'll die with you, Daws, we've always known that was an option. But the last thing you hear in this life is going to be my voice saying, 'I told you so!'"

"That's fair," Daws acknowledged, the smile still plastered on his face. "Let's finish this together, shall we?"

Lori nodded and Yrris pulled at my sleeve.

"He's going through with it, isn't he? He's going to try and fight the First?"

"It appears that way, Lady," I affirmed.

"Does he not respect my opinion? Does he not believe me? This isn't only a lost battle we're talking about. If he actually manages to draw the personal attention of the First, it could mean the end of his entire world. The First could very well decide to handle things personally and destroy everything on this planet. His power has no limits! He's not like the others! Phillip, make him understand!"

"It won't work," I responded simply.

"How do you know if you refuse to try?!" She demanded.

"Because nothing is stopping me from trying."

"That doesn't make any sense!" she sobbed. "Why can't my translator make sense?"

I felt truly sorry for her in that moment. Her world had turned upside down and sideways several times over in the last day or two, and her only link to her new world was a man who couldn't even explain his own limitations. Worse, even that link would soon disappear and she would be left to fend for herself, assuming she survived what happened next.

"Daws," I began, giving Yrris at least some effort on my

part. "The Lady Yrris is quite insistent that you are underestimating your enemy. She says he is not limited in his power like the other Tanniks. She would have you know that you risk your entire world if you draw the personal attention of the First."

The words came smoothly and freely. Never once did I feel the slightest resistance. So although Daws furrowed his brow, made a show of thinking, and had me translate to Yrris his sentiments of respect and gratitude for her opinion, I knew that he never once deviated from or even questioned his chosen course.

Chapter 27

Paranoia is a dangerous and insidious disease. Few things can so thoroughly twist a person's soul against those closest to him.
–Musings of the Historian

Though a somber mood pervaded our inner council, the soldiers were quite enthusiastic as they divided up to see to their various duties. As discussed, some of them would be acting as heralds, spreading the news of what had happened and the greatness of Daws, their savior.

The bulk of them would go to the Vortex, once again set up a perimeter, and try to hold the hotly contested ground. A chosen group would accompany Daws and the rest of us through the Vortex.

"Am I gathering the people to the Vortex to come through?" Yrris asked. "We were interrupted before. There are so many more people, entire other settlements we haven't even been able to contact. Are we going to leave them behind?"

To my surprise, Daws nodded once he understood the question.

"Yes, we are. I know we accepted your people as refugees and started the immigration, but things have changed now. We're not going to move your people into this world, we are going to make your own world safe by eliminating the Tanniks."

She looked as sorrowful as a hound dog having its food taken away, but she did not argue.

The preparations were accomplished quickly and without much embellishment. It was mostly coordinating supply. Each soldier was prepared with enough food, water, flares, and ammunition to make a significant stand, even if separated from the group.

The trip through the Vortex again struck me with how familiar it was. There could be no mistake. Whatever it was I went through when the horizons shifted during my travels, this Vortex was operating on the same principle.

It bothered me on a personal level that people weren't more curious about it. Lori had mentioned that she had people working on the mystery, but that was it. Everyone else in our party seemed to accept it as a fact of existence. Granted, the portal hadn't been open long before there were much bigger concerns to occupy people's minds. Still, it seemed like a crucial piece of the puzzle to overlook.

The land looked exactly as it had the last time I had come through. The dingy red clouds still streaked a dim sky.

"Lady Yrris?" I drew her attention and motioned up at the sky. "Is this day or night? It looks the same as the last time I was here."

She jumped in with an explanation.

"I have heard of settlements several weeks' travel to the south that have days like you have in the other world, switching from full dark to full light, back and forth. But here, it changes very gradually. We are in the lighting season, and it will continue to get brighter and brighter. The sky will be a pale violet when the light is full, then it will start to darken again."

Lori grabbed my arm, anxious to hear the translation of the answer. When she had heard it, she turned to Daws.

"We must be near one of the poles," she explained. "Day and night would only change as the planet rotates around the sun."

"Wouldn't it be colder?" Tratch interrupted. "Our poles are completely uninhabitable they're so cold."

"It should be colder," Lori admitted. "My guess is that it has something to do with the odd atmosphere we're seeing. I'd have to take several samples back to the labs for analysis, but I can only guess that its makeup allows for a more even heating of the planet."

"Fascinating," Daws commented, then turned to me. I waited for him to speak, but he didn't. The silence quickly turned awkward as moments turned to minutes.

"Sir?" Lori asked, being the first one to break in our little group. I had been waiting for Daws to speak, and he had been waiting for me to become uncomfortable. He would have waited a long time. I am a patient man.

"Just waiting to see if 'Phillip' here is ready to make his play," Daws said my assigned name with all the sarcasm he could pack into the two syllables.

"My play?" I asked, amused.

"Yes." Daws was still calm, but there was irritation flowing underneath the exterior. "Your move. Are you a Tannik or aren't you? Did you really expect us to believe that you were a passerby in all this? Your ability to understand and be understood by both peoples, the subtle pressure we've felt inside our own minds to trust you, and our inability to even document your appearance.

"All of these things point towards some sort of psychic power, which speaks of magic. More than that, Lori told me about how you survived the attack by Shriver. Did you think she would forget such a thing?"

I shrugged. "Kind of, yes."

"Well she didn't!" Daws snapped. "Above all these things, we've all been watching you and you've never been scared once. You weren't scared when Death came through the Vortex, even when everyone else was terrified. You weren't frightened when Shawen was executing soldiers like she was stomping mice. You weren't even scared of Shriver when he was actively attacking us. You acted concerned, but you should have been panicked.

"So who are you?" he pressed. "Are you the First? Perhaps some other Tannik with mind control powers? Changing what we see, perhaps?"

"Is that what you think?" I asked. "That I'm the First or a similarly powerful Tannik?"

"That's one theory, though it's not the only one. Kip? Anything to add?" Daws switched his eyes to the surprised man, who clutched his plant closer to his chest.

"Me?" Kip whimpered. "What do I have to do with any of this?"

"Maybe nothing," Daws answered. "But Tratch, Lori, and I had a little meeting about you three. Lori was the first one to suggest that we could already have a Tannik among us, one clever enough to use stealth and incursion instead of invasion.

"Hours later, all evidence pointed to you, Phillip. You are clearly not human. Lori has suggested that you might be even more intelligent than her, and I would have told you that was fully impossible.

"That's when I suggested that it was a bit too perfect. If we were looking for a Tannik who could affect perception and was truly brilliant, they wouldn't leave so much evidence behind. They would push suspicion onto another. That's when we started looking at Kip."

I smiled. I couldn't help myself. I knew where this line of suspicion was going and I was loving every moment of it. Kip, however, was failing to see the humor in the situation. He was literally trembling at the knees, Chuck's leaves quivering. His mouth opened and closed, trying to find some defense, but failed. Daws pressed the attack.

"His record was perfect, beyond suspicion. His history was corroborated by countless people and official records. There wasn't a single anomaly, neither good nor bad. If we tried ourselves, we could not have crafted a more average person."

"Hey now!" I interrupted. "That seems a little harsh."

Kip shot me a panicked look. More than anything else in the world right now, he wanted to be seen as an average person and didn't appreciate me challenging the assumption.

"Why is Daws yelling at Kip?!" Yrris asked, concerned.

"Daws thinks that one of us is a Tannik spy, possibly even the First himself. He's saying that Kip is average and inconsequential in every way, which makes him the absolutely perfect suspect for a spy."

"What?" Yrris was flabbergasted. "Kip isn't a spy! He was there when I came through and I was the first to come through the Vortex. He's a sweet man. This is ridiculous!"

I chuckled. "If you think this is ridiculous, wait to see what comes next."

Daws glared at me, daring me to speak again. I gladly accepted the dare.

"Lori suspected me, that's understandable enough. I have my quirks. You went even more paranoid and pointed your finger at poor Kip here. I wonder who Tratch suspected."

Eyes turned to Tratch and he looked suddenly sheepish.

"I thought it was the plant," he mumbled.

I clapped in delight, laughing loud and deep. It was a good, soul-cleansing laugh.

"Of course he thought it was the plant!" I crowed. "This is the sick glory of paranoia. When you start trying to guess who you'd least suspect, that's a line of thought that doesn't end."

My jovial manner ceased suddenly, my eyes flashed anger, and my tone turned cold.

"It's exactly that kind of fear that turns leaders into despots, butchering their own people over imagined offenses. Power and fear is a gruesome combination, Daws, enough to twist a man into a monster. If you fall into this path, you might make the Tanniks start to look good after a while."

Daws glared back at me, unflinching under my accusations.

"It sounds like you know something about that, Phillip," he shot back. The barb cut deeper than I expected.

"I might," I confessed, suddenly subdued. "I've heard rumors."

"This is pointless," Daws decided aloud. "If any of them were the First, this would have been a perfect moment to strike at us, here on their own turf. Even if they were a lower Tannik, we've already taken out three of their most powerful rivals. They would have moved on by now."

"Why keep us so close if you thought we were dangerous?" Chuck asked. Kip was still too scared to speak for himself, but somehow he summoned the courage to translate for his plant.

"You went to war, but you know so little about warfare," It was a condescending statement, but Daws's smile was genuine. "Have you heard the saying, 'Keep your friends close, and your enemies closer"?

"If you were the First, then we had to learn as much about you as we could, hopefully learn enough to predict when you would attack and how. We have also been feeding you false information, though I still won't say exactly what information was false.

"If you were a minor Tannik using us to get rid of rivals, then we were allies, at least for a while, and we were willing to accept any help you might give along the way. We have no experience with the Tanniks, so for all we knew, you could have been working in our favor this whole time, weakening their power; maybe altering their perceptions to our advantage."

"Did you hear that, Kip?" I beamed at him. "We've been powerful allies all this time."

"I was trying to help," Kip grumbled, visibly disappointed at discovering how much more had been expected of him.

Daws hung his head, his shoulders shaking. It took me a moment to realize that he was trying to hide a laugh. No doubt he was coming to terms with the absurdity of the fact that he had been dragging an insane, average citizen and his houseplant along during the most dangerous and vital campaign of his entire career.

He finally succeeded in fighting down his mirth and raised his head, though a broad smile still stretched across his face from corner to corner. To my surprise, he went and hugged Kip, careful not to crush Chuck in between them.

"You did help, Kipland. I thank you for your service, soldier. You are a credit to our entire nation."

Kip stood a little taller. I was touched by the scene, though I noticed that I still didn't get a hug and a "thank you." Apparently I was still under suspicion.

"Phillip," he turned to me. For a moment, I wondered if I had been mistaken and was actually going to get a hug as well, but my first impression was the correct one. "Would you please ask Lady Yrris how we might find the First?"

I turned to ask the question, but Yrris already had a rant of her own ready to unleash.

"They thought you were the First? Or Kip? Or the bloody plant?! Right now Kip is looking like the sanest one in this group! And I'm as crazed as the rest of them for going along with this idiotic plan.

"The First needs no subterfuge, no strategy. He is completely indestructible. My grandfather speaks of a time when the mightiest Tanniks of his day, more powerful even than Shawen, rebelled against the First, tried to kill him by surprise.

"They had even arranged witnesses, so that the entire world would know who the true masters were. My grandfather, as leader of the slaves, was present. He said the Tanniks rained furious destruction down on the First. The sand all around him was burned, melted, and twisted into nightmarish wounds on the earth, so intense was their unleashed fury.

"Most of the humans started running as soon as the initial attack had begun, but my grandfather stood his ground and watched. He said you could hear the laughter through the smoke. The First shrugged off their attack like it was a joke.

"Then he attacked the rebellious Tanniks. It wasn't angry, furious, or even fast. My grandfather said it couldn't even count as a battle. It was a series of calm executions, like a man stepping on insects to hear the crunch."

Chapter 28

How can I know so much and understand so little? It is the primary frustration of my existence.

–Musings of the Historian

Too impressed for sarcasm or jokes, I translated the story word for word for Daws and the rest of the team. Lori looked sick. Daws and Tratch were impressed, but not scared.

"Then he won't try to sneak up on us," Tratch commented, sounding satisfied. "I was worried about having to look over my shoulder."

"You guys are crazy!" Kip commented, though he didn't turn and run through the Vortex, which would have been the logical course of action after hearing such a thing.

Scouts and messengers were dispatched to the various slave settlements. News of the death of Shriver, Shawen, and Death would be public knowledge soon. Daws's soldiers teamed up with people from Lady Yrris' party. The locals would bring the news and tell the stories, the soldiers would act as guards, scouts, and eyes for Tratch as he looked for defensible positions.

Our primary target was the First, but we knew that plenty of lesser Tanniks were still at large in the land. From Lady Yrris, we knew that they didn't concern themselves much with the human population, leaving such matters mostly to Death, but they would still be dangerous if encountered.

More than anything else, they were looking for indications

of the First. If what Yrris had said were true, he would be coming at us straight on, we would see him coming and have some time to react.

We didn't have to wait long.

A lone soldier came scrambling back from one of the parties we had sent out. They had been sent back to Lady Yrris' settlement to check for anyone who had been left behind.

"The First!" he shouted, before he had even reached us. "The First is headed this way!"

"Shut up!" Tratch snapped at him irritably. "Pull yourself together and give us a real report, man."

The harsh tone worked wonders on the man and he straightened up, his hands unconsciously brushing at the dirt on his uniform. He had seen something traumatic, that was clear, but this was an elite soldier. He was ashamed for his momentary lack of discipline.

"My apologies, sir," He snapped a smart salute, then launched into his report. "We'd reached the village about an hour after leaving this location. We found a man standing in the center of the village. The locals immediately started panicking and trying to pull us away. They were saying something over and over again, it sounded like 'pyervus.'"

Yrris started at the name and tugged on my sleeve. "That means 'the First.'"

Daws understood her agitation without translation.

"So they were able to recognize him," he noted. The soldier nodded. "Could you see anything different about him?"

"No, sir," the scout replied. "He looked like a regular person, though I will admit that something felt off."

"Off, soldier?" Tratch scolded. "Explain yourself."

"Sorry, sir!" The soldier straightened up even stiffer. "The air felt heavy, like it was getting harder to breathe, and there was energy in the air, like the static on a standard issue blanket, you know the type, sir, when it comes out of the package…"

"I do, soldier," Tratch cut him off. "Continue your report."

"Well, when we walked up, he was looking the other way, so I couldn't see his face. We started to retreat, like the locals were urging us to. You had ordered us not to engage, sir, we weren't being cowardly."

"I know you weren't," Tratch responded, though it was said out of irritation, not a desire to comfort. He knew the courage of the men he had brought, now he wanted the report finished.

"So then he just up and waves his hand, like he was saying goodbye to us. Then the buildings were gone, flattened, and everyone was dead except for me."

"What killed them? The falling buildings? How were you able to avoid the blast?" Tratch pressed, peppering the poor soldier with questions.

"The buildings didn't kill anything, sir. I don't know if he even meant to knock them down, it was like him using his power at all sent out shockwaves. The people died all around me, fell down like toys. Nothing killed them, they were just gone, like he'd snatched the life out of them directly. Then he was there in front of me, calm as anything, standing there like we'd been having a conversation the whole time.

"He asked me if I came through the Vortex…"

"You understood him?" Lori interrupted this time. "He was speaking our language?"

"I can't say I thought much about it, miss, but I understood him fine."

Daws and Lori exchanged a glance and Lori's eyes flitted toward me for half a second. The soldier jumped back in on his report.

"I didn't answer him, but he didn't seem to mind, he nodded like I had told him something. Then he was gone and I was alone, there with all the fallen buildings and dead bodies, sir. I've been hustlin' back here ever since."

"Pull everyone close back through the Vortex," Daws ordered. "Those who are far away should stay there until we can come back for them. We don't know how fast this guy can move, so let's act as if he'll be here any second."

"A wise choice," a deep voice commented. The air suddenly felt heavy and electric. None of us had to turn our heads to see what was there.

The First had arrived.

"BACK THROUGH THE VORTEX!" Daws roared and leapt through himself, being the closest. The nearby guards, Kip, Tratch, Lori, and the surrounding guards scrambled over themselves on their way through the Vortex.

I spun on my heel, turned to flee...

...and tripped.

Musty earth filled my nostrils and the sounds of panicked retreat filled my ears. Then all was silent.

"What have we here? A clumsy guard?" The deep voice held deep amusement and a toe prodded my side. A pulse of power ripped through me, but found nothing to catch on.

A grunt of confusion was followed by another burst of energy. It was like nothing I'd felt before. I'd been wounded in a variety of ways before, but for one fraction of a second, my entire body was completely consumed and gone. It was incredibly disconcerting. I pulled myself back to my feet and turned to face my attacker, noting the sand that had been burned to glass several paces in all directions around me.

The First took a quick step back, gasping.

"What is this?! Nothing could survive that! It would rip the soul from your body!" The deep, confident voice was gone. True amazement was written plainly on his face. He leaned in and peered at me, trying to pull some answer from my eyes.

"You are not from their world." It wasn't a question. "And you are not from mine. None of us are capable of creating such a thing."

He moved forward carefully, putting each foot in front of the other cautiously, one hand raised in front of him, as if approaching a poisonous snake.

"Such craftsmanship!" he marveled. "Even the flaws… yes, the brush strokes are there, even they are intentional. Who are you?"

"I am the Historian," I offered weakly. I could remember few times when I had felt so vulnerable. It was the only true statement I could offer. His face twisted in befuddlement.

"I hear the truth in your words, and long ago, I heard legends about such beings, though somehow you're saying it wrong. You've changed something, somehow. You are not punished?"

"Not that I am aware of," I answered. "Though I am limited."

He nodded, enthusiastic with his agreement.

"Oh yes, you would have to be! Can you imagine…?" He trailed off, lost in his own thoughts. It took a moment before he returned to the present.

"Why are you here, then? You can't have been allowed to

join these people." He waved a hand dismissively towards the Vortex. "Unless that is how they managed to kill my pets."

I shook my head.

"As far as I know, I haven't changed this story yet. Though I have been deeply involved, I sense that nothing I've done has changed anything. The end of this story is sure, regardless of my interference."

He smiled. It was a dark thing, equal parts power and cruelty.

"I understand, stories would be sacred to your kind. You might have helped them a little, but you don't have the power to act directly, not without consequence. Are you ready to see the end of this story?"

The air grew even thicker and it became harder to breathe, though I technically didn't need to. Power pulsed from every cell of this being. I knew his confidence in that moment. The end of this story was always going to be the ultimate conquest of both worlds by this creature.

Unless I did something.

I reached out my hand and he stepped back, startled. The resistance hit me, painful and intense. I gritted my teeth and took a step, trying to force my way through it. The First smiled.

"That is incredible. I wonder if your masters have any idea of your will."

I took another step. Nausea rolled over me, but it was a distant discomfort. The real agony was within my own mind. It was confusion and mental pain as excruciating as a red-hot knife being twisted in my own skull.

"Save your strength, Historian. You might be able to shift a leaf with that puff of air, but you will not budge an oak."

216

I fell to my knees. This time it wasn't an act, as my earlier stumble had been. Then, I'd only wanted an excuse to get a closer look at the First, maybe a word or two before the final confrontation. I had gotten what I had wanted, but it was nothing I could have expected.

I relaxed and the pain faded. The First was right. I couldn't interfere in the story to such an incredible degree. Even my most intense effort could only make minor shifts. There was no way I could outright eliminate a character of such importance.

I hung my head and turned to the Vortex. The First put a hand on my shoulder, comforting me in a condescending moment.

"It was honorable that you tried. I am as far above you as your masters are above me, it is the natural order. There is no shame in bowing to it."

Anger flared in me at his dismissive arrogance, but there was nothing I could do about it. I wanted to ask him what he knew about my "masters," but I could barely speak, exhausted by the effort I had expended to try and change the story.

We walked through the Vortex together like that, my head hung and his arm around me. We stepped through to a familiar sight. Daws had the room set up for his guest. The time difference had given them ample time to prepare. Two chairs faced each other in the center, Daws sat in one and he motioned the First to sit in the other. Behind Daws, chairs were arranged in a semicircle.

The original team was there, finishing together, how we had started. Tratch didn't sit, but stood to the left and just behind Daws, a communicator held to his lips, though he didn't seem to be talking. I wondered what devastating attack he was ready to unleash on this location should things get out of hand.

I saw a window with ropes already hanging out of it to the side of the room. That was our fastest retreat, but having felt the power of the First, I knew it was a hopeless gesture.

Directly behind Daws sat Lori, then Yrris was next to her, then Kip. Even Chuck had his own chair for the final council. There was an empty chair that I guessed was for me. I felt flattered at the confidence that implied, them expecting that I would somehow escape the First and make it through.

The First had made the same conclusions and shoved me toward my assigned chair before moving towards his own.

"Thank you for sparing my translator," Daws said, not bothering to get up to welcome the newcomer.

"Translator?" the First scoffed as he sat down, looking toward me. "Have a little dignity, Historian. You should have been a god to these people, not an errand boy."

"So you two know each other?" Daws asked. "I see you have the same power with languages. Are you on the same side?"

"An eagle cannot be on the same side as a fish," the First scoffed. "I know him only by reputation. I learned your simplistic language through my pets who gathered information for me before they died. The power of a Historian is his alone.

"You and I work to rule worlds," he spoke to Daws. "His masters could wipe them from existence with a thought. Know your place, Daws, you are here as a visual aid, nothing more. I would have his masters know that I dealt fairly with your kind as much as I was able."

"What are you calling fair?" Daws asked.

"I will allow you to serve me and live," the First announced it grandly, sitting tall in his chair, a king bestowing mercy.

Chapter 29

Love can forgive any sin but betrayal.

–Musings of the Historian

"So in return for our slavery, you would let us live?" Daws clarified.

"That is correct," the First affirmed.

"And you are really that powerful? We would have no hope of survival if we opposed you?" Daws asked in an oddly relaxed tone, as if discussing umbrellas or a sporting match.

"That is also correct," the First nodded, pleased at the cordial nature of the negotiations. "I have seen all of your technology through the eyes of my pets and I can assure you it would all be meaningless against me.

"Do you need a demonstration? Lower forms often have trouble grasping abstract ideas. Perhaps I kill half of this world's population first before we negotiate."

"Just don't hurt the plant," Daws shot back. "We'd take that real personal, wouldn't we, Tratch?"

"Downright offended, sir. I think we've all become fairly fond of our little mascot."

"I couldn't agree more," Daws continued to drawl lightly. I looked from Daws to Tratch and back again. Something was very odd. Both of them were far too relaxed. Lori, Yrris, and Kip were positively terrified. Yrris was green and Lori looked like she was about to throw up. Kip was pale and even Chuck seemed to wilt from the power crackling in the air off of the person of the First.

The First himself was momentarily stunned by the absurd direction the argument had taken. He looked to me for some sort of explanation, but I had none to give.

"How about intelligence?" Daws asked, continuing the bizarre conversation. "Are you smarter than us, too? Maybe we could outsmart you like we did your attack dogs. We're pretty bright, you know, aren't we, Tratch?"

"Brilliant, sir," Tratch echoed. "Especially with Lori on our side. She's one sharp cookie, that one."

The First was moving now from bewilderment to irritation. A sneer twitched at the side of his mouth.

"You little rodents," he hissed. "You try my patience. You would compare your feeble intelligence with me? With ME?! You're barely sentient! I have lived for millennia, I have discovered the secrets of magic, sculpted my world with its power, and raised pitiful humans like you to levels of power they never had the imagination to dream of. Your intelligence means nothing, your weapons mean nothing. Submit now or I will feel perfectly justified in wiping your flawed race from your filthy planet."

"You know," Daws again spoke to Tratch, ignoring the First. "I think he means it."

"I'd say so, sir. See the way his forehead gets all tense there. Sure sign he's ready to wipe us out."

"You say the words, but lack the reverence, you swine," the First snarled. "With no challenge, it's been a long time since I enjoyed killing someone, but I'll enjoy killing you."

He stood and Daws stood with him. Then Daws, all of his joking manner gone, spoke.

"I'm sure you would, you false god. And I will submit myself, my people, and my whole planet to your rule if you can answer me one question. If you cannot, you die here and now. Would you take that wager?"

The First smiled in true amusement.

"Every time I think I've got humanity figured out, you surprise me again. Is this some kind of insanity? I am tempted to continue this little act, if only for the entertainment. Very well, ask your question, you have won yourself another few seconds of life with your audacity."

"Who opened the Vortex?"

Confusion flashed across the First's face. It was all Daws needed to see.

"Tratch, close the Vortex."

Tratch muttered into the communicator that he still held to his mouth and the Vortex evaporated away like a mirage.

The air cleared instantly, the electric charge suddenly clear. The First collapsed into his chair, gasping for air like some sort of fish on land.

Daws sat back down on his chair with much more grace. He pulled a knife calmly from his waist, and without any preamble or warning, plunged it into the thigh of the First.

The scream was something truly primal. It was the unrestrained roar of a being that hadn't felt pain in thousands of years, if ever.

The scream ended and the First sucked in a new breath. In that moment, his eyes locked onto Daws and the true significance of the act settled in. The second scream was pure fear, a horror that gripped the very soul.

"You and your monsters killed a lot of my people. I couldn't let you escape all punishment." As calmly as he had been acting, the anger burning inside Daws now surfaced. "I've enjoyed your pain, but you're too dangerous to let live."

He drew his sidearm smoothly and pointed it at the First.

"Wh…" The First managed to cut his scream off long enough to raise his hand, scramble back in his chair, and start to speak before Daws pulled the trigger. A single carbon fiber pellet, propelled to supersonic speeds by an ignited spoonful of compressed gas, left the barrel of the gun, traveled the intervening space, and shot through the skull and brain of the First.

The intricate balance of life was unable to recover from such trauma. The lights and life behind the First's eyes vanished and he slumped forward in his chair, dead.

The room was silent in shock. Even Daws, who had been acting nonchalant the entire time, sank in his chair a little, his shoulders sagging. Tratch put a hand on his shoulder, a silent moment of triumph between comrades.

"What was that?" Kip was the first to break the silence.

Daws stood and walked over to the First, doing a quick check for any remaining signs of life. Finding none, he shoved the First from the chair and the body slumped unceremoniously onto the floor. Daws sat down in the newly vacant chair, facing us. He launched into his explanation like a sports star retelling his finest moment.

"A few researchers I trust came to me a while ago, reporting some consistent errors in their experiments. Everything was going as expected, except that there was a minute amount of energy being lost.

"We only became aware of this because of the more advanced measuring equipment we've recently developed. Even

222

more interesting, the effect was always consistent in specific locations, but if you moved locations, say to a different lab, the effect would change, and become consistent at a different level.

"None on that team were able to figure out the cause, so I quietly reached out to some other teams, proposing the problem as a hypothetical. It wasn't until I pitched the idea to our theoretical physicists that I got a viable answer."

"The missing team," Lori whispered. Daws nodded his confirmation.

"They suggested a leak. Something was drawing power away from our world, possibly through some sort of dimensional rift. I can't say I understood everything they were saying."

Daws shrugged sheepishly at that.

"Anyway, I connected the last set of scientists with the first set and sequestered them away from everyone else. I gave them the task of figuring out where the leak was, if it could be stopped, and finally, if it could be reversed and used to power our own technology.

"What they came up with was a device. Rather than trying to shut the leak down, they would purposefully feed power into it, isolating the specific frequencies that seemed most likely to be lost. We had expected some sort of heat or light to focus around the rift. We had plain clothes officers scouring the area we thought most likely.

"We never expected anything like this," he confessed. "The Vortex opening created an entirely new set of possibilities. When Yrris displayed her magic for the first time, I knew where our lost power was going. Somehow, they managed to harness the difference in energy between their world and ours, channeling it through their bodies or their world to produce the incredible effects we saw.

"While we fought the Tanniks, the scientists were able to calculate the physics of the Vortex. Once they knew its exact location, they were able to figure out how to send out a canceling wave that would seal the rift, at least as long as the wave was being transmitted."

Lori stood and walked over to Daws, standing in front of him.

"You didn't tell me," she whispered, though we all could hear.

"I…" Daws began, but there was no reason he could give. He'd left her out of his plans because he hadn't needed her for that part.

"How long did it take them to figure out how to close the Vortex?" she asked, cutting off his stammered attempts at explaining why he had left her out. Daws was happy to get back to his narrative.

"Not long at all! Only a few hours. The trick was making sure we could open it again. They'd already done most of the calculations. Once they had the specific location…"

The sound of the slap reverberated in the small room. Tratch took half a step forward, but did not interfere.

She slapped him again, hard. Daws did not raise a hand to stop her, and Lori didn't stop. She managed four more hard slaps before hissing and stopping from the pain in her own hand.

"How could you?" she sobbed. "All those soldiers, all those people, Yrris…"

She broke off, overwhelmed by her own emotions.

"Oh Yrris." Her hand went to her mouth. "I was the one who helped her sacrifice her people.

"And I…" She started again, her wet, bloodshot eyes wide with horror. She couldn't finish the sentence. She slapped him one more time, as hard as she could, then stormed out.

Kip picked up Chuck and walked out as well, leaving only a rude gesture behind for Daws.

Daws stood, stunned for a few moments, his hand raising to his face, the fingers tracing lightly over the hot red skin.

"She'll come back," he muttered.

"No, she won't." I was on my feet now. "You went too far, paid too high a price, and she's gone for good. It'll be months before you truly understand how much you needed her, and maybe years before you realize that you loved her."

Chapter 30

The first indication of maturity is knowing when to keep your mouth shut. The final proof of maturity is knowing when not to.
-Musings of the Historian

Daws lowered his hand from his face, grimacing at me.

"Tratch, wait an hour, then reopen the Vortex. Take Lady Yrris and the body through. Let's spread the word. Let's also establish a beachhead on that side of the Vortex. We can't always rely on luring them through the portal, we'll have to have a way of defending ourselves on the far side. Leave the communicator for me."

Tratch saluted smartly and scurried away to follow orders. Daws sat back in his chair and rubbed at his temples. This should have been his greatest moment of victory, the First literally laying defeated at his feet, but he looked a little sick.

I left him where he was and went over to Yrris, who was still sitting, reeling from the shock of what she had seen.

"I'd love to know your thoughts, Yrris," I prodded gently, urging her from her reverie.

"You were right," she began. "You were right about everything. Daws really was more dangerous than the First. I can't believe he's gone. He was a god."

She was still stunned, staring at the body of the First, lying like discarded trash on the ground next to Daws. The man had pulsed with power and majesty, had ruled with uncontested might over his entire world, but all of that had been as nothing compared with Daws's machinations.

"What have you learned?" I asked.

"That a person can be mighty." She unconsciously sat a little straighter in her chair as she said it. "I've spent my whole life comparing myself to the Tanniks based on magic and the ability to destroy. I thought myself so feeble. Now Daws has butchered them like cattle and he has no more magic than a dirt clod."

"Very true," I commented, though Yrris wasn't done.

"We've been so afraid. We've let them use us and discard us like animals because we feared them." The bitterness was rising in her voice as she reflected on the humiliation of her people's history. "We didn't even try to fight. We thought it was hopeless.

"But that's not the only thing you were right about, Phillip." She said it like an accusation. "You also tried to warn me about Daws. You spoke about his hunger for power and I didn't listen."

"It's all right…" I started to comfort her, but she threw it right back at me.

"I was right not to listen!" she spat. "You think the First could have been brought down by an honorable man? Are you so naïve that you don't see the deals we have to make as leaders? I see the monster in him, Phillip, as you predicted. But he's our monster.

"He has saved us. Nothing you can say about his ulterior motives can change the fact that he has ended the tyranny of the Tanniks. I and my people will reverence him and all of this team for the glory they have wrought."

"I realize that, but you still…" I started to interrupt and she raised her hand to silence me.

"As I remember what he has done, I will also remember

what he has taught me," she continued. "And if the power sickness takes him one day, as you claim it will, we will put him down. We won't be afraid of his power. We will remember that he was the one who taught us to be brave. And when he dies at our hand we will weep. We will mourn for years over our friend."

With that, she rose and left the room.

I walked back to Daws and sat down in the chair he had left, facing him as he had faced the First.

"Why did you do it?" I asked him. "If you could have closed the portal at any time, why did you keep it going after people started dying? I know why you let Death run amok, it gave you the perfect setting for taking over the country, but why continue the charade?"

Daws looked up at me. His eyes were bloodshot.

"The First called you a Historian. Is that like some sort of record keeper?"

"Something like that," I responded.

"Then you must not be a very good record keeper. You're not very observant," he threw at me, tapping his chest oddly with his index finger, as if pointing at something.

"That's the first time anyone's ever accused me of that," I responded. "And I've been around quite a while and been accused of a great deal. I don't have much time for guessing games. The story is over and the pull to walk away will come very soon, I expect.

"Tell me why you wanted to fight the Tanniks. Were you really that intent on saving Yrris' people? You could have done that more easily by bringing them here and…"

"HER BUTTONS!" he shouted at me, unleashing some of his frustration at me. "I saw her buttons, you thick clod."

228

Then I remembered. Yrris had iron buttons on her dress. They were simple and plain, but for a world starved for metal, they would have shone like gold, and gold they hadn't seen at all.

"I figured if a slave could be wearing iron buttons like it didn't mean a thing, it must be abundant indeed. Our iron supply rules the people, as we need all we can get for our crops and supplements. Without it, the people become anemic and weak. Our last great war was fought over the richest iron mines on the planet. That's why I kept going.

"If I could control an endless iron supply, everything would change. We'd have enough for our people with no recycling. With that, I could practically buy the other country--we wouldn't even have to invade. Though if we did have to invade, we'd have iron on our side. My scientists have told me about things they could invent if they had enough iron that would astound you, Phillip."

"They really wouldn't," I commented drily. He waved me aside irritably.

"You don't understand. We're talking about more than just mining, wealth, or even conquest. We're talking about a new future for this world and theirs. Technology would explode, the citizens of both worlds would live better than any past generations have ever known!"

"And who would lead them to this new and glorious future?" I asked with a smirk.

"Me!" he exploded. "And don't you dare judge me. Who else had the vision? Who else is actually trying to unite the nations? People are too bogged down, trying to figure out which person should be in charge of burying the trash that they never take the time to dream of better."

"Well then, I guess this is the time for congratulations," I remarked. "You must be very happy."

He only scowled at me in response and I continued.

"You wielded love and hate on either hand and only saw them as weapons. Now you have achieved everything you ever wanted. I've never liked you much, Daws, but that's something I wouldn't wish on the worst of men."

He looked truly miserable as he looked up at me. There was a part of me that recoiled at the sight. Something within me saw a possible version of myself.

"You promised me a favor," I stated. "It turns out you do have something I want."

"What do you want?" he asked, sounding exhausted.

"I need you to get on that communicator to your physicists. I want them to tell me everything they know about the Vortex and the science that formed it."

"You wouldn't understand it, and it doesn't work if there's not a rift already present," he answered, though he was already toying with the communicator, raising the correct channel.

"Let me worry about that," I responded. He spoke a few words into the communicator and handed it to me.

I listened for half an hour as a dry voice on the other side drawled on about light cones, energy flows, and quantum instability. When the lecture had finished, I lowered the communicator.

I walked to the window and looked down. Yrris had her hand on Lori's back, comforting her. In that moment, I understood why I hadn't been allowed to translate for Yrris on that one occasion. That moment was when Lori and Yrris began their friendship. They would be strong together, strong enough to even rival Daws.

I felt ashamed I hadn't seen it earlier. I had seen too much to have so casually overlooked the power of personal connection.

Daws had recovered from Lori's angry exit, at least on the surface. He again saw himself as the clever future ruler of two worlds, not as a lonely man sitting in an empty room.

"What now?" he asked, drawing my attention back into the room.

"Now I wander on," I said. He was already shaking his head.

"No, no, no. I'm not done with you yet. I demand answers."

"I wouldn't mind some myself, but we're both likely to be disappointed there."

"You and I shared a moment of honesty once, let's have one more. Do you understand me?"

"More than you'd like," I answered. He only nodded and continued.

"Am I powerful?"

"More than you should be."

"Are you powerful?"

"I've heard rumors," I told him for the second time that day.

"More powerful than me?"

"You aren't even in my league."

"I thought so," he said, raising his hand. I hadn't seen the sidearm, hadn't realized that he had been holding it ready since he had shot the First. He fired without hesitation, his hand steady. The pellet burst through me as it had with the First. Unlike the First, I was completely whole immediately after the pellet's passing.

I smiled at Daws, but anger coursed in my heart. There was a deep, deep part of me that sneered at his efforts, and was offended that he would dare challenge me. I pushed it away, disturbed. It was too close to what I had seen from the First.

Daws drew himself up, scared now, and fired another shot. His aim was unerring, but the second shot had no more effect than the first.

I channeled my anger and leaned into it. Maybe I couldn't stop the First, but I would change this story, if only a little.

"You're a great man, Daws," I began, the resistance already starting to tug at my essence, as if it sensed my intention.

"And here I thought you didn't like me," Daws hissed and fired another harmless shot.

"I only said that you were a great man, I never said you were a good man," I clarified. "But let me help you there, Daws, in the only language that'll reach you. I will be watching you."

The resistance flared within me, scraping layers from my mind. I gritted my teeth against it, disguising the gesture as anger towards Daws. His eyes widened and he reached up and flipped the switch on the barrel of the gun.

He paused only to step one foot back, bracing himself for the recoil. Then he pulled the trigger and I was washed in flame. I walked through the brilliant colors of the fire, appreciating the distraction from the turmoil going on in my own head.

The gas ran out and the flames died. Some corner of my mind recognized that Daws had started backing away from me. With the sound of the weapon gone, I continued my attempt at shifting the story.

"And if you oppress this people, if you enslave them, if you crush them when they try to resist your will, then I'll be back. I'll come back, Daws, and take everything away from you."

Reality seemed to be tearing away from me, ripping at my

232

very soul. Things were shifting, I could feel it, but making the story move cost me deeply. I felt unseen forces start to pull me away, the horizons blurred, even though I could see no horizons inside the small room.

Daws wasn't moving away any more and through my clouded senses, I realized his back had hit the wall.

"Do not risk my fury, Daws," I hissed through grit teeth. I reached out and grabbed his head, drawing it close to mine, forcing him to look directly into my eyes. He squirmed as some part of him rebelled at the wrongness of it, sensing on some level that I didn't belong in his reality.

I was starting to slip away, I could feel it and fought against it, but there wasn't much I could do.

"Tell me what you want," he begged, truly horrified for the first time in his life. "How can I prove myself?"

"Be a generous leader. Take care of Kip and those like him." The room was blurred. Even Daws was a vague outline, though I felt him nod by my hand on his neck. The universe swirled and I felt myself slipping. Only time for one more thought.

"And Chuck could use some more sun."

Then it was all gone. Soft, wispy clouds drifted above me in the sky. I was walking, as if I had already been on this path a long time. The pain of my effort lessened with each mile that passed under my bare feet. I felt good about my meager contribution.

I wasn't naïve enough to believe that Daws would usher in a new era of peace and prosperity to both worlds based on our conversation, but he would remember my warning during dark times, and fear would nudge him to make the right choice.

It was difficult to make the change. I called it resistance, but in truth, it felt like weakness. Some part of me knew that this wasn't my story. Still I can't regret the pain or the effort. Some stories need to be changed, and this was an important story...

...this was a story about you.

About the Author

Lance Conrad lives in Utah, surrounded by loving and supportive family who are endlessly patient with his many eccentricities. His passion for writing comes from the belief that there are great lessons to be learned as we struggle with our favorite characters in fiction. He spends his time reading, writing, building lasers, and searching out new additions to his impressive collection of gourmet vinegars.